GOLD MEDAL MURDER

NANCY DREW
girl detective®

THE HARDY BOYS
UNDERCOVER BROTHERS®

Available from Aladdin

GIRL DETECTIVE ®

NANCY DREW

AND THE

UNDERCOVER BROTHERS ®

HARDY BOYS

Super Mystery #4

GOLD MEDAL MURDER

CAROLYN KEENE
and
FRANKLIN W. DIXON

Aladdin
NEW YORK LONDON TORONTO SYDNEY

This book is a work of fiction. Any references to historical events, real people, or real locales are used fictitiously. Other names, characters, places, and incidents are the product of the author's imagination, and any resemblance to actual events or locales or persons, living or dead, is entirely coincidental.

ALADDIN

An imprint of Simon & Schuster Children's Publishing Division

1230 Avenue of the Americas, New York, NY 10020

First Aladdin paperback edition July 2010

Copyright © 2010 by Simon & Schuster, Inc.

All rights reserved, including the right of reproduction in whole or in part in any form.

ALADDIN is a trademark of Simon & Schuster, Inc., and related logo is a registered trademark of Simon & Schuster, Inc.

NANCY DREW and colophon are registered trademarks of Simon & Schuster, Inc.

NANCY DREW: GIRL DETECTIVE is a trademark of Simon & Schuster, Inc.

THE HARDY BOYS MYSTERY STORIES is a trademark of Simon & Schuster, Inc.

HARDY BOYS UNDERCOVER BROTHERS and related logo are registered trademarks of Simon & Schuster, Inc.

For information about special discounts for bulk purchases, please contact Simon & Schuster Special Sales at 1-866-506-1949 or business@simonandschuster.com.

The Simon & Schuster Speakers Bureau can bring authors to your live event. For more information or to book an event contact the Simon & Schuster Speakers Bureau at 1-866-248-3049 or visit our website at www.simonspeakers.com.

Designed by Sammy Yuen Jr.

The text of this book was set in Meriden.

Manufactured in the United States of America/0510 OFF

4 6 8 10 9 7 5

Library of Congress Control Number 2010921709

ISBN 978-1-4424-0326-0

ISBN 978-1-4424-0327-7 (eBook)

0312 OFF

CONTENTS

CHAPTER 1

NANCY

EN GARDE!

The school gym was quiet and empty. The late afternoon sunlight drifted in through the windows high overhead. I stood still in a sunbeam, waiting. I was breathing hard. I held my sword defensively in front of me.

I'm in trouble, I thought. *Big trouble.*

Suddenly, my opponent rushed at me out of the dark! I blocked a vicious swipe at my head and stepped back to avoid a lunge at my torso. I was able to keep from getting hit, but just barely, and I was rapidly being pushed back across the gym. My opponent was breathing strong and steady, almost as though she hadn't even worked up a sweat.

On the other hand, my ragged breathing and the

clang of sword-on-sword echoed through the cavernous empty gym. School was long over. There was no one around. My attacker forced me backward, step by step. Soon I would be pinned against the wall of the gymnasium.

It was time to try something daring. I leaned forward, making an easy target of my head. She'd be stupid to pass up this opportunity.

Sure enough, I heard the *whip* of her blade swinging through the air, on a collision course with my face. At the last possible second, I ducked low and scooted forward, lunging at her unprotected stomach. For a moment, I thought I had her. But she was impossibly fast. Her sword was down and parrying mine before I'd even gotten close to her.

We strained against each other, our swords connected at the hilt. I grunted, pushing with all my might. Then my opponent twisted her wrist too fast for my eyes to follow, and my sword went flying through the air. A half second later, I felt the point of her blade at my neck.

"Yield!" she said.

Applause drifted in from the open gymnasium door, where the figures of George Fayne and Bess Marvin—my two best friends—had appeared.

"Well done, Lexi!" Bess yelled.

I grabbed my throat and made thick choking noises.

I fell to the ground, shuddered a few times, and then lay still, pretending to be dead.

My opponent lowered her blade and executed a short bow.

"You're as good an actor as you are a fencer, Nance!" yelled George.

Lexi Adams, my opponent, classmate, and one of the world's best female fencers, removed her mask. Her curly red hair tumbled free, wildly framing her heart-shaped face.

"Hey now," she said. "She's getting a lot better."

She reached a hand down to help me up. It was hard to feel bad about losing to Lexi. She wasn't just the star of the River Heights High Fencing Team—she was the youngest woman on the American Olympic Fencing Team. She was a world record holder at the age of nine. I'd been getting lessons from her all year. I didn't think I'd be joining her on the Olympic team anytime soon, but you never knew what sort of skill would come in handy when working on a case. Plus, it was a pretty good workout.

"That was great!" Bess came running over. With her love of fashion—and her model-gorgeous good looks—Bess was the last girl you'd expect to find hanging out in the school gym. But she and her cousin George were both avid exercisers, although George preferred hiking outside to being in the gym. But they could agree on one thing: rock climbing. Which is where the pair had just been before wandering in at the end of our fencing match. I could tell by the chalk dust on their hands and the special climbing shoes they both carried. River Heights High had an indoor climbing wall, and they both made good use of it.

Of course, Bess worked out while wearing a matching pink headband, wristbands, and sweat socks, which coordinated perfectly with her lemon yellow terry cloth short-shorts. She looked like a model from one of those chic athletic-wear catalogs. George, on the other hand, was favoring her usual many-pocketed cargo shorts. I never knew what kind of gadgets she had on her, but they often came in handy when I was working on a case. George's tech savvy was unparalleled.

"So are you nervous about the Olympics?" George asked Lexi. "The LA blogosphere is really blowing up about it." From one of her pockets, George pulled out her cell phone. In terms of abilities, it was somewhere between a supercomputer and a video editing studio. It made me feel like I was still tapping out Morse code.

"Look!" she said. "Someone posted your River City High yearbook photo today!"

"What?" said Lexi. "Ugh. My hair was terrible in that photo."

"The price of stardom," said Bess. "Besides, you always look cute, you know it."

4

"Even though I've never been to LA, I'm excited the Olympics are happening there this year," said Lexi. "Makes me feel like I've got a hometown advantage. Plus, it means I can keep practicing here right up until the games start, which makes my dad happier."

Lexi's father was also her fencing coach, and he was notoriously protective of her—like a stage mom with a sword.

"You're going to love it!" I told Lexi. "It's a really fun city."

"I don't know how much of it I'll get to see," she replied. "I mean, there are the Olympics to think about."

"Olympics, Schmo-lympics," said Bess. "Think about the fashion! You've got to hit Rodeo while you're out there. I'll give you a list of stores to check out." She laughed.

"I don't know, Bess. If what the Internet says is true, Lexi is going to be a little too busy with a certain swimmer to go anywhere." George waved her phone around, showing a picture of Lexi and Scott Trevor with their arms around each other. Lexi blushed.

Scott was the darling of this year's Olympics, a multi-gold-medal swimmer with the body that went along with being in a pool for six hours a day. His face was on everything, from cereal boxes to swimwear. I'd even heard a rumor that he was going to be hosting *Saturday Night Live* this month!

He was also Lexi's boyfriend, a secret they'd been trying to keep for almost a year.

"I'm excited to get to see him! We've both been training so hard, it's been almost impossible. This is a big year for him—he's set to break the record for the most individual gold medals held by any athlete in the world!"

Lexi's face suddenly darkened. The smile faltered on her lips. George and Bess were cooing over photos of Lexi and Scott on George's phone, but I couldn't help noticing that something seemed to be wrong. Call it my detective sense—I smelled a mystery.

"Is something wrong, Lex?"

"What? No. No, it's—it's nothing, really."

The tone in her voice caught Bess's and George's attention. Bess threw her arm around Lexi.

"Spill it girl," she said. "Boy problems? Talk to me."

"Oh no! Everything is fine with me and Scott. I'm just worried about him. There's been some . . . stuff happening recently."

"Stuff?" I said. Something about her voice made me worried.

"Is this about the threats?" George broke in.

"Yes—how did you know?"

George waved her phone again. "The Internet knows everything."

"The Internet might, but I'm in the dark," I said. "What's going on?"

Lexi sighed and looked down.

"It started a few months ago. I mean, star athletes get a lot of fan mail in general, and some of it's always the crazy stalker type or threats or whatever. You just learn to live with it. But Scott started getting really intense, crazy hate mail as the Olympics got closer and closer. He just laughed it off and tried to focus on the swimming, but . . ."

"But what?" I asked.

"Last month, someone stole his laptop and put all his information online—cell phone number, e-mail address, credit cards, everything. He had to quit the gym he used, move, get a new number. It was a mess. And the letters started saying there was worse to come if he didn't drop out of the Olympics now."

"Has he gone to the police?" I asked. This was serious stuff. He needed some protection.

"Yeah, they're looking into it, but they haven't found many leads. The Olympics assured him there would be good security, though, and he lives in LA anyway, so he won't have to travel or anything."

Lexi grew quiet, but she didn't make a move to leave the gym. Something else was clearly on her mind.

"Lexi," I said. "You've been getting threats, too, haven't you?"

"How did you know?!" She shot a look at George's phone. George shook her head.

"That's Nancy for you. She knows more than the Internet—especially when it comes to mysteries. So what's the deal?"

"I didn't want to mention anything. My dad—he's so protective, you know? But I've started getting e-mails that say if Scott doesn't quit, I'm the one who's going to get hurt."

"Lexi! You have to tell someone." Crazed fans had been known to hurt stars, even to kill them. Lexi was putting herself in terrible danger by not reporting these threats, even though it was likely they would never amount to anything.

Lexi bit her lip for a moment. A host of expressions struggled to cross her face. Finally, she forced herself to smile.

"Oh, I'm sure it's fine. Just nerves. This stuff happens all the time."

She tried to laugh, but it came out hollow.

"Lexi, I think—" I started to say something, but she cut me off.

"Listen, don't mention this to anyone, okay? I've got to go shower. My dad will be here any minute to pick me up."

With that, Lexi ran out of the gym. I stared at her retreating back. A thought started to form in my head.

"I know that look," said George. "What are you thinking, Nance?"

"Nothing," I said. "But you know . . . I've never seen the Olympics. And it's in the country this year. It would be a shame to miss it."

Bess looked at George, a smile spreading across her face.

"Rodeo, here I come!"

They gave each other a high five.

"Well, if you think about it, Dad, it's important that I go to the Olympics. I mean, who knows when they're going to be in the country again, right? And as a civic-minded citizen, I think it's important to support any event that promotes global collaboration!"

Carson Drew was a big-time lawyer, and a firm believer in taking part in important events. He was also my dad. Right now, those two parts of him were battling it out over whether I should be allowed to go to the Olympics. I'd cornered him after dinner—he washed the dishes; I dried them.

"A week on your own in LA Nancy? I don't know."

"I won't be on my own—Bess and George are going to come too. Plus, Lexi will be there. You always say how important it is that I support my classmates."

I was pulling out all the stops on this one. Something told me that Lexi was going to need my help—even if she wasn't able to ask for it yet. Of course, I wasn't going to mention that to Dad.

"All right, all right!" Dad threw up his soapy hands. "You can go."

"Thanks, Dad!" I gave him a big hug. I hated hiding anything from him, but this was important. I knew it.

"Just be careful with whatever case it is you're working on. I expect a full briefing *and* daily check-in calls, you hear?"

I laughed. Of course Dad wasn't fooled. But he was letting me go, and that was all that mattered!

CHAPTER 2

JOE

BIG HAIR, BIGGER WEAPONS

"Frank! A little help here!"

I stepped to the side, trying to get into a more defensive position. I stumbled a little, though, as my foot encountered the edge of the narrow wooden bridge on which I was standing. I nearly went down to my knees. I could hear the guy behind me take a quick step forward, but he dropped back when I regained my balance. I noticed a strange buzzing noise, getting louder by the second, but I couldn't tell what it was coming from. The two guys in front of me were watching me closely, waiting for the right moment to charge. They were dressed like refugees from a bad eighties movie—big frizzy hair, spiked leather jackets, and plastic framed sunglasses. What was with gangs and the terrible matching outfits?

Didn't they realize it just made them look silly?

All three were carrying very, very big sticks. Sticks with bits of metal shoved through them—sharp and rusty nails. Those made them look a little more serious.

"Frank! I haven't had a tetanus shot in years so you need to get over here right now!"

Where was Frank? And what the hell was that buzzing noise? The only thing that was keeping these three dudes from rushing me was the two of their friends who were already unconscious at my feet—Tweetle Dumber and Tweetle Dumbest, who'd walked right up and let me knock their lights out. These ones, however, were being more careful, and it was only a matter of time before all three of these guys came at me at once. I was good—well, heck, I was great—but if the three of them attacked me at the same time, I'd give them fifty-fifty odds they could take me.

The two in front of me had noticed the noise as well. It was now incredibly loud. They glanced behind them, and I got ready to charge them. It was my best chance. I was just about to start running when a motorcycle came flying over the hill, straight for the bridge. The two guys scattered to the sides. I heard two loud splashes as they landed in the river below.

"Jump on!" yelled Frank. Frank slowed the bike just enough to let me leap onto the back. As my arms wrapped around him, he revved the engine again. He popped up on one wheel and drove straight for the guy who had been creeping up behind me on the bridge. The thug stood his ground for a second, but when it became clear that Frank was fine with running him over, he followed his friends into the river.

"See ya, suckers!" I yelled as we zoomed out of sight.

For a few minutes, Frank drove in silence, trying to get us as far from the gang's stomping grounds as possible. Then he started to slow down.

"Keep going!" I yelled. "Once they get on their bikes, they'll catch up to us in no time."

"Don't worry," said Frank. "I removed all the starters before I took this one. They're not going anywhere."

"I'm glad you weren't out wasting time while I was fighting the baddies," I said.

"Speaking of which—where are the plans?"

"What plans?"

The bike skidded to a stop so fast we nearly flipped over.

"JOE! The plans we were supposed to get from these guys—the ones they stole? Our whole mission?"

Frank sounded kind of peeved. I let him twist in the wind for a second.

"Just kidding big bro. Got 'em right here." I patted the bulge in my pocket. "Now, let's get out of here. I have hair spray all over my hands from fighting those dudes."

For a second, I thought Frank was going to make me walk back to ATAC headquarters.

With everything wrapped up for ATAC, the only thing left on my weekend plan was to play ZOMG Kill 3, my favorite video game. I'd already won it twice, but until ZOMG Kill 4 came out for at-home play, it was the best game out there. My hands still felt vaguely sticky, even though I'd showered. We were in Frank's room, since that's where the game player was. Frank was lying on the floor, studying . . . something. What else was new? I heard the doorbell ring downstairs, but over the opening music of ZOMG 3, I barely noticed it.

"Boys!" yelled Aunt T. "You shouldn't have ordered pizza! Dinner is going to be ready soon."

"Pizza?" I said to Frank.

"Did you . . . ?"

I shook my head no. This could mean only one thing.

A moment later, a familiar face loomed in our doorway.

"Hey, Frank. Hey, Joe. Anybody order one mission with extra danger?"

It was Vijay! Vijay Patel was a fellow ATAC agent, who specialized in intelligence and undercover operations. He'd been our contact for new missions before. He was also a big video game geek, so I loved getting to work with him. He always had the latest handheld games to play while we were on stakeouts.

He flipped open the lid of the pizza box he was holding.

"This will give you guys all the details on the case. I've got to get back to headquarters."

Inside the box was a familiar looking disc. I was pretty sure that was ZOMG Kill 4! Some of our missions came disguised as video games. After we watched the briefing, they worked just like the real thing! This was awesome. Vijay must have arranged it.

There was also, however, a pizza with mushrooms and anchovies. Gross!

"Can you take that back with you?" I asked him, pointing at the pizza.

"And give us a hint on what the mission is?" added Frank.

"Sorry, no can do. It would look suspicious if I left with the pizza. I think your Aunt Trudy is already a little annoyed that I interrupted her soap opera watching. And all I'm saying about the mission is this: I'll see you guys in LA!" With that, Vijay bounded back downstairs.

LA? I was liking the sound of this. LA meant two things to me: beaches and movie stars. Perhaps even movie stars on the beach. In bikinis. Sweet.

Frank grabbed the disc from the pizza box, as well as a slice.

"Ew," I said.

"Pizza's pizza," he responded, and he took a big bite.

I flipped the lid of the box closed so I wouldn't have to smell it.

I took ZOMG Kill 3 out of the console and we popped the new disc in.

The opening scene was of a tall, muscular young man in a Speedo and goggles getting out of a pool.

"That's Scott Trevor!" said Frank. "People say he's the fastest man on Earth! Or, well, in water." Frank was an avid swimmer and was on the Bayport High School swim team. I vaguely recognized Scott from a poster Frank had on his wall.

As Scott waved to the crowd in the video, a voice-over on the video began to explain exactly what Frank had just said. Turned out he had, at twenty-one, already won six Olympic gold medals and set multiple world records. He'd also begun to receive numerous death threats, all focusing on the upcoming Summer Olympics in LA.

"Yes!" said Frank. We high-fived. Going to the Olympics had always been a dream of ours, and now ATAC was sending us!

The camera panned across the new Olympic buildings that had been built for the games.

Up until recently, the threats had been a little less common that what he generally received, but nothing out of line. But a recent burglary at his house, combined with more frequent—and violent—threats, had made the Olympic officials nervous. The games brought in a huge amount of publicity, as well as controversy over human rights abuses in participating countries and fights about the money used to build the stadiums. The last thing they needed was more negative publicity.

Suddenly, Vijay appeared on the screen.

"Hey guys! So, for this mission, it's going to be the three of us out in LA."

This just kept getting better. We'd had a few recent bad matchups with other agents on missions, including one who had tried to kill us in the Florida Everglades. But working with Vijay was always awesome. He was as good an agent as he was a fun person.

On the TV screen, Vijay continued to break down the mission for us. He would mostly be working remotely, in charge of the computers and communications end of things. This mission was going to be spread over a lot of territory filled with a lot of people, and we couldn't be everywhere at the same time. Our primary goal was to keep Scott safe.

"As for you two," Vijay continued, "Frank, you're going to be posing as the head of the Bayport chapter of the Scott Trevor Fan Club, as well as an amateur swimmer—and the winner of a recent "Biggest Fan" competition held by Sportztime, the mega–sports website and TV channel. As the winner, you've been granted the right to follow Scott around throughout the entire Olympics, with a backstage pass that should get you entry to pretty much everywhere except the women's locker room."

"Joe, you're going to be Scott's new personal assistant. Anyone who wants to talk to Scott is going to go through you. As will all his e-mail, phone messages, etc. If anyone tries to slip anything to Scott, you're going to intercept it."

"Woo-hoo!" Frank and I shouted in unison. Almost as though he had heard us, the Vijay on the screen held up one hand.

"There is, however, one catch. Scott will know Joe is with ATAC, but Frank, you're going to be in deep cover on this mission. No one—not even Scott—will know that you work for ATAC. You two will have to act as though you don't know each other. Most of your communication will have to go through me. These threats could be coming from anyone, even someone close to Scott, and we need to have someone that Scott can't accidentally give away."

Frank and I looked at each other. This was going to be tough. We worked together really well. It was, in fact, what made us the best agents in ATAC. Working separately was a whole different story. We'd be able to check in, but still. This mission was going to try our abilities to the limit.

"Good luck guys," said the recording of Vijay. "I'll see you out in LA in three days. Until then—enjoy ZOMG Kill 4!"

CHAPTER

FRANK

LA BITES

Since ATAC hadn't provided us with a cover story for our parents, Joe and I came up with one of our own. We were both on the swim team at school, and it wasn't hard to make up a story about a field trip to LA for the Olympics. We faked a permission slip for our Mom to sign. If our dad, Fenton Hardy, hadn't known the truth about ATAC and been able to cover for us, it probably wouldn't have worked. But with him on our side, it wasn't too hard to get our mom and aunt Trudy to believe that Bayport High was sending us to Los Angeles for two weeks, all expenses paid.

We had a few days to prepare before we left for LA, which Joe spent playing ZOMG Kill 4. He said it improved his "hand-eye coordination," his "strategic survival skills," and his "likelihood of surviving an all out zombie/human war." Mostly, it seemed to give him calluses on his hands and kept him from sleeping at night. By the time we left, he looked as much like a zombie as any one of the bad guys in the world of ZOMG.

I decided to spend some time doing research on Scott Trevor, since I was supposed to be his number one fan, after all. I was already a little familiar with him. It was hard not to be, really. His face was everywhere: cereal boxes, TV commercials, ads for shoes. I never understood the shoe ads. You didn't wear shoes for swimming. But I guess a famous face can sell anything.

I watched videos of him at the 2004 Olympics, where he'd beaten his own world record in the one hundred meter freestyle event. I memorized his times, his height, and even his favorite food (pad thai with lots of tofu—he was a vegetarian). If he had been a subject in school, I would have gotten an A+. By the time we were ready to leave, Scott Trevor had even begun to appear in my dreams! And boy, were those some strange dreams.

Joe and I took separate flights from Bayport to LA. He would be meeting up with Scott first, in an official ATAC briefing so that Scott would know exactly who and what he was. The next day, I would be presented to Scott as the winner of the "Biggest Fan" competition held by Sportztime. Sportztime was currently filming a documentary about Scott, and our first meeting was to be captured on camera. I just hoped that we had the case wrapped up before it aired!

The taxi from the airport dropped me off outside of Scott's giant house/complex, which was right outside LA, along the water. In all the interviews, Scott said he preferred swimming in the ocean to the pool, unless he was racing. I was struggling up the walkway when a voice yelled out to me.

"Wait! Stop! Go back." A man came running out of the house toward me with a microphone in his hand. He was exactly what I thought people from LA would look like: tan, tall, blond. Though in his forties, he was obviously still in good shape. A cameraman came running after him. I almost did a double take when I recognized Vijay, who pulled the camera away from his eyes just long enough to shoot me a quick wink.

"Hi," I said. "I'm—"

"Frank Carson, I know." Carson was the fake last name ATAC had given me for the mission. The man with the microphone continued talking. "I'm Alex Smothers, founder of Sportztime. And I wanted to get you exiting the taxi for the doc, but now the taxi's gone and the shot's ruined. Oh, well, let's get you inside."

Alex Smothers had been an Olympic swimmer in the 1980s, and had managed to turn his fame into a lasting sports media empire. He also didn't seem to breathe between any of his sentences. If he could swim as fast as he could talk, no wonder he had been so famous! I'd done some reading on him, too, since he was the host of the "Biggest Fan" competition I had supposedly won. The competition had been real enough—ATAC had just rigged the results for me.

Scott's house wasn't just big, it was a complex. There were wings and levels and gardens, all climbing up a hill in some prime waterfront real estate. We entered through the gym. And this wasn't some basement home gym, with a few weights and one of those "total workout machines" that were advertised in my spam mail. This was a full private gym: treadmills, barbells, weight machines, sauna, and Jacuzzi. And, of course, a full-size Olympic pool.

Scott was doing laps when I entered. I'd seen the same thing in a lot (a *lot*) of television clips, but seeing him in person was a whole different experience. The way he moved was unreal. It was as though the water parted to make room for him. He was so at home in the water it was like he was a merman or a dolphin— something definitely not human or meant to live on the land. Before I'd even begun to grasp how fast he was moving, he had already crossed the length of the pool and was climbing out near me.

A man ran over to hand Scott a towel. In my mind,

I checked him off from the list of people and names with which ATAC had provided me. It was Lee Singh, Scott's manager. Singh had "discovered" Scott at the age of twelve, when he'd been Scott's coach on his middle school swim team. He had been a close friend and advisor ever since, though it was only recently that he'd taken up the position of manager as well. There were a number of other people in the room as well: Joe, in his role as Scott's new personal assistant; Lexi Adams, Scott's girlfriend and fellow Olympic athlete; and Lexi's manager, who looked (from the strong resemblance) to also be her father.

With a broad smile on his face, Scott walked over to me.

"Hey man," he said. "I'm Scott Trevor. I hear you're my number one fan. Good to meet you."

I stuck out my hand, and he grabbed it firmly in both of his. As we shook, I could feel Vijay going in for the close-up. For a moment, I didn't know what to say. It wasn't hard to pretend to be a nervous fan around Scott. He was pretty awe-inspiring.

"Uh, yeah! That's me. Your fan. I mean—it's great to meet you, Scott. Sir. Mr. Trevor."

Scott laughed. "Call me Scott," he said. "So I hear you're a swimmer too?"

"Yeah," I said. "A little."

The conversation halted. Neither of us knew quite what to say. Luckily, Alex stepped in.

"Scott, what sort of advice would you have for Frank, as an aspiring swimmer, and all your other fans out there?"

I stepped aside as Scott began to talk into the microphone about the importance of daily training and really "going for it." I didn't pay a lot of attention. It was clear that I had served my purpose for the documentary, and my job now was to stand here and smile. Occasionally, Alex would direct a comment my way, like "Isn't that interesting?" I would nod and smile, and he would turn back to Scott so they could discuss their shared experience of being Olympic gold medal swimmers. Joe and Vijay took turns making faces at me when no one was looking, and I tried not to burst out laughing.

At one point, I could feel Scott getting a little tense. I tuned back in to the conversation.

"Now, up until recently, you were romantically linked to your former manager, Elisa von Meter," said Alex. "But there were some people who maintained that you and Lexi were always together, and that Ms. von Meter was a red herring. Would you care to comment on that?"

"No," said Scott firmly. Watching the interview, I could see the angry look on Lexi's manager's face. Yup, no doubt about it—that was her dad.

"Well," Alex started again, "how long have you and Lexi been together?"

Lee Singh stepped between Scott and the camera.

"I'm so sorry," he said. "But we're running a little behind schedule, and I'm afraid Scott has to do his warm down and eat. He's on a strict schedule these days. I'm sure you understand the pressures of being an Olympian, right, Alex?"

Alex didn't look pleased, but he knew how to take a hint. He put down the mic and gestured to Vijay to stop filming. While they began to pack up their gear, I asked Scott if I could use the restroom.

"Oh, yeah, sure. You could just go in the locker room, but it's a little gross in there. So take the third door over there, go through the long hallway, up the stairs to the next floor, and it's the fourth door on the left off the living room."

This was what I'd been hoping for. Aside from meeting Scott officially, my other job this afternoon was to help hide a series of video cameras around his house. Vijay would be monitoring the cameras from the Communications HQ he had established off-site, so if anything went down, we'd know about it.

It was also a great chance to check out the rest of Scott's house. Unlike the training facility, which was full of equipment and people, the house was quiet and empty. Not empty like he hadn't moved in, but empty like he wanted it that way. Everything was white, from the walls to the carpet to the furniture. In the hallway, there was a giant white vase filled with white flowers. The staircase was a spiral staircase, all white, made out of iron, and it seemed to go all the way up to the top of the house. Sun streamed down from a skylight somewhere far above.

The place was insanely neat. Everything was in its place and there was no dirt anywhere. But it couldn't have been too hard to keep it that way—there was nothing to get out of place. He didn't even have any books, at least not that I could see. No wonder Scott could swim for hours a day—he had nothing else to do!

It was hard to place the cameras in such empty rooms, but I did the best I could. They were small, about the size of a quarter. I hid one among flowers and another few on the staircase. I tried to find Scott's bedroom, but to no avail. There were doors everywhere, leading to more white hallways and empty rooms. It was a house you could easily become lost in.

Finally, I found myself in the living room Scott had mentioned. It was ginormous! But everything in it was white, making it hard to tell where the floor ended and the walls began. Maybe it was all an optical illusion, and it wasn't as big as it looked? Or maybe it was even bigger. It hurt my eyes to try to focus on anything too carefully.

About halfway across the room, a flicker of motion

caught my eye. I looked down. Had something brown just flitted underneath the couch I was passing? I paused for a second, but saw nothing. I started to walk forward again.

And then I heard it. The telltale sound of a hollow rattle, followed by a slight slithering. Rattlesnake!

If I was close enough to hear it rattling, that meant I was close enough to be in danger of being bitten. I stood as still as I could, trying to pinpoint where the sound was coming from. It must have been under the couch I was standing next to. Or the little footstool. Or the small decorative table. Or . . . The more I looked around, the more I realized the room was full of furniture and things that were hard to notice before, because everything in the room was white. The snake could be anywhere!

Correction: Make that snakes. I heard a second rattle, somewhere off to my right. Then a third, close by the second. It wasn't unusual for snakes and other animals to find their way into new homes in LA while they were being built—there just isn't much room for wild things to live anywhere, so they like empty houses—but something told me that this had just gone from coincidence to attempted murder. And while I may not have been the intended target, I just might end up the victim.

I looked around. Close by was a white statue of a

tree, about three feet tall. It was solid at the base, and I felt pretty sure no snake could be hiding underneath it. Very, very slowly, I climbed on top of it. With a little bit of height, I could see around the room. Right off the bat, I spotted two more snakes lazily slithering between pieces of furniture. This room was a reptilian minefield! There was no way I could chance walking back.

I looked at the door I had entered. It wasn't that far away. I began to calculate the distance. If I leaped from this statue to the back of the armchair, and stepped from there onto the dining table, and from there to the love seat . . . It looked like I could make it back without ever touching the floor.

The first part was going to be the hardest. The arm-chair was a good four feet away, and if I landed wrong, I'd go flying to the ground, where I'd be lucky if I just broke my neck and wasn't bitten by a snake. Or three.

I psyched myself up to jump.

"One . . . two . . . three!"

I leaped. I hung in the air for a split second, and then my right foot landed hard on the wooden back of the chair. Immediately, the chair tipped back onto two legs. I brought my left foot down onto one of the arms, hoping to balance the weight and keep from falling over entirely. For a second, the chair teetered, trying to decide whether to go back to standing on four legs or fall all the way over. I windmilled my arms, trying to balance as best I could. Then the chair landed back down. I let out a sigh of relief. Safe.

After that, the rest of the trip was easy. I made it to the door without ever stepping once on the floor. Once in the hallway, I raced back to the training center.

"Help!" I screamed, as soon as I got through the doors. "Snakes! There are snakes in the house!"

It was kind of fun to act like a frightened teenager, instead of having to be the calm one who solved the problem. But it seemed like I did it a little too well. At first, no one believed my wild story of a living room full of rattlesnakes.

Thankfully, Joe came to my rescue.

"Scott," he said, his hand touching Scott's shoulder, "you never know. Maybe he did see something. We should probably call pest control, just to be safe."

Joe's presence was a good reminder that Scott was in danger. Scott nodded and had Lee make some calls.

Thirty minutes later, two guys in stiff denim overalls entered the house with nets and canvas bags. Fifteen minutes later, they came back with not one, not two, but *nine* rattlesnakes. Everyone breathed a sigh of relief—until one of the men dumped his bag on the floor! Snakes poured out everywhere.

One of the snakes landed right by Lexi. She screamed and brought her foot down on its head. Then she leaped backward.

"What the—" yelled Scott.

"Don't worry," said one of the wildlife control guys. "They're not dangerous."

He bent down and grabbed one of the snakes by the head.

"In fact, they aren't even real."

He flipped the snake over and popped open a lid in its belly. Out dropped two double-A batteries. They were robots. Incredibly convincing, totally harmless, robots.

"Looks like someone's playing a prank on you," the guy said. "Got a younger brother or something?"

Younger brother—or stalker? Everyone laughed and tried to pass it off as a silly joke, but I met Joe's eye and knew he was thinking the same thing I was. Someone was trying to psych Scott out.

CHAPTER 4

NANCY

ROAD TRIP!

The suspense was starting to kill me. It was just barely after sunrise on the morning we were set to leave for LA, and my dad had just dropped me off in a small parking lot near the highway that led out of River Heights. Between words of advice ("Always have money for a cab, just in case" and "Don't bet against the Russian gymnasts"), he adamantly refused to tell me why he was taking me . . . wherever it was we were going.

For the last two weeks, the only thing that George, Bess, and I could talk about was our upcoming road trip. That's right: road trip! Through a mixture of begging, pleading, and promising to do a million chores when we got back, we'd gotten our families to agree to let us drive on out to Los Angeles. Ever since I'd gotten my sky blue hybrid-electric car—nicknamed "Twinkle"—we'd been talking about taking a road trip somewhere, and this seemed like the perfect time. What could be more all-American than taking a road trip across the country out to see the Olympics?

Besides, the three of us were the perfect trio to go on a road trip. Bess could fix any car, anywhere, at any time. George had so many GPS devices and other electronic navigation tools that she was almost part robot. And I, of course, had Twinkle.

Or rather, I *had* Twinkle. A week ago, he'd disappeared from the street outside my house. I almost had a heart attack, but my dad told me not to worry about it—Bess and George had a surprise for me. No matter how hard I begged them, they wouldn't tell me what the surprise was. Not that I saw much of them. From the moment the car disappeared, Bess and George were gone too. Once I saw Bess on Main Street, wearing an oil-smeared jumpsuit, but somehow still looking her model fabulous self. She scurried in the other direction when she saw me coming, though.

I sat on my luggage in the parking lot, blowing on my big Thermos of coffee, just waiting for the moment it was cool enough to chug. I was not a morning person. This coffee was a medical necessity.

Suddenly, I heard the sound of a car approaching. I shaded my eyes with my hand, and saw a sky blue car headed directly at me. It looked almost like Twinkle, if Twinkle were a convertible. Then I saw the heads of the driver and passenger. There was no mistaking the mass of blond curls beneath an Audrey Hepburn–style scarf-and-sunglasses combo or the no-nonsense brown ponytail. That was Bess and George . . . which meant that was Twinkle!

"Surprise!" they yelled as they pulled up beside me.

I couldn't say a thing. I just stared at the beautiful car beside me. They'd not only made Twinkle a convertible, but they'd also redone his paint job and managed to knock out all the dings and dents I'd put in him along the way. He looked beautiful.

"What? How? I mean, wow!"

"You like it?" said Bess.

"You know it!" I replied, running my hand against the smooth medal side.

"I remembered how much you loved the fleet of hybrid-electric cars they had down at The Wetlands—so we decided to make you one of your very own!"

The Wetlands had nearly spelled the death of Bess, George, and me—as well as our friends, Frank and Joe Hardy. But they were right; the cars were nice. Maybe the nicest thing about our time there, other than seeing the bad guy behind bars.

"We made a few other modifications." George smiled. She began to point at various things along the dashboard.

"This is an input line for your MP3 player. I mean, what's a road trip without good music, right? And this"—George pulled out the key and held it up so I could see the new ring it was on—"is an auto starter. Now you can turn it on from a hundred feet away!"

This was awesome! No more waiting for the car to heat up on cold mornings—or trying to find it in large parking lots. Sometimes, when I was on a case, I forgot little details like where I had parked.

George tossed the keys at me and scooted into the backseat.

"What are you waiting for?" yelled Bess. "Hop in!"

They didn't need to tell me twice. I took the driver's seat.

"Los Angeles, here we come!"

The next five days were pure pleasure. We took a leisurely route, stopping at every tacky road side attraction, mini–petting zoo, mammoth cave, natural wonder, and mysterious rock formation between River Heights and Los Angeles. We camped out most nights to save money. The weather was perfect—sunny during the day, but cool at night so that it was easy to sleep. It was almost relaxing enough to help me forget that we were on our way to one of the craziest cities in the country, where a friend of mine was receiving death threats!

On the afternoon of our fifth day, we started to hit

traffic—according to our guidebook, that was a sure sign that we were near LA! The smog started too. For the time being, we decided to put the top back up.

"Okay, girls," said Bess. "Get your star-spotting glasses on. I'm not leaving here without at least a few autographs."

"You know, if we head down toward Venice Boulevard, I hear there are a couple of movie studios down that way. You'd be sure to get some autographs there," said George. "And I could stop in and see if I could get a tour of the animation studios. You wouldn't believe what they're doing with CGI these days! It's incredible."

They were both so excited, they talked as though they had just downed six shots of espresso each. I hated to cut them off, but we had a few things to attend to first.

"How about we find the hotel, and then go sightseeing?"

"Right. Sorry, Nancy." Bess blushed.

"I'll get us directions." George whipped out her smart phone, and soon we were headed deep into the heart of Los Angeles, looking for the Starlet Grand Hotel. When we found it, it was every bit as "grand" as we could have hoped. There was a red carpet leading up a set of marble steps, with two golden lion statues roaring on either side. My dad had a friend in LA who owed him a few favors from work that they had done together in the past, and he'd pulled some strings to get us a suite here. Not only was it a beautiful building in one of the ritziest areas in LA, it was also the same hotel where Lexi was staying!

At first, I thought it was strange that Lexi wasn't staying at the Olympic Village with most of the other athletes. When I'd asked her about it, she'd blushed and stammered. Finally, she'd admitted that it was her father's idea. He didn't want her to stay anywhere near Scott. Her dad was superprotective when it came to Lexi dating. Even though the men and women were staying in different areas of the Olympic Village, he wanted Lexi somewhere even farther away, preferably where he could stay and keep an eye on her.

On the plus side, it meant I could keep an eye on her too. We'd managed to score the suite directly below Lexi. I'd wanted something on the same floor, but the Starlet was pretty booked up due to the Olympics, and we were lucky to get anything.

"Look at this balcony!" said Bess as we settled into our rooms. "You can see the entire city from here!"

"Look at all the neon!" said George.

The famous skyline of LA was just beginning to come to life as the sun went down. It was a beautiful sight. And the guidebooks told the truth—the sunset was a thousand different colors: red and gold and orange and yellow, but also green and blue at the edges.

Bess and George would be sharing the larger of the two bedrooms, which had two full-size beds. The smaller room only had a twin bed, but I liked the privacy. Sometimes, when on a case, I've been known to stay up way late making up theories and going over the evidence, and I didn't want to disturb Bess or George.

Once we had everything squared away, we headed upstairs to find Lexi.

"Room 1407—here it is!"

I knocked on the door. No answer, but I could hear someone moving around. I knocked again. Nothing.

"Maybe they're not—" Bess started to say, when the door was pulled open a crack.

"What?"

David Adams had never been the friendliest citizen of River Heights. And even though Lexi had been in school with the three of us since kindergarten, he didn't seem to recognize—or even really look at—Bess, George, or me.

"No autographs," he said briskly.

He went to shut the door, but I shoved my foot in it.

"Ow!" That door was heavy! But so long as the door was still open, I had the chance of getting in touch with Lexi. "Mr. Adams, we're friends of Lexi's! From River Heights!"

Mr. Adams didn't look convinced. He went to close the door again, but then a voice called out from behind him. "Nancy? Is that you?"

Lexi came running up behind her dad. Reluctantly,

he opened the door all the way. Lexi's face appeared next to her father. The resemblance between the two of them was strong, except when it came to their expressions. David looked angry and suspicious. Lexi looked excited, but also worried.

"Remember, Dad—I told you some of the girls from school were coming to watch the Olympics."

Lexi shot me a look as she spoke. I could take a hint. Ix-nay on the death threat talk while her dad was around. I couldn't blame her—the last thing she needed was for her father to have one more reason to be overprotective. Although, given the evidence, perhaps he had reason to be overprotective.

"We're so excited to watch you compete, Lexi," said Bess.

"It's going to be awesome," I added. "We just got in and were thinking of getting some dinner. Want to come with us?"

Lexi looked at her father, her eyes pleading with him. He was silent for a full ten seconds. Ten long, quiet seconds. Finally, he shook his head yes.

"So long as you girls stay in the hotel. And remember, you have training bright and early tomorrow! And don't go seeing that *boy*. I swear, he's ruining your training schedule. Good for nothing . . ."

Lexi shut the door on her father's grumbling. We were all silent for a second, then burst out laughing. Of course that was her dad's biggest worry—Scott!

The Starlet's restaurant was named Dinner Theater. Like many things in LA, it revolved around Hollywood. There were photos of famous actors everywhere. Many were photos of the actors actually at the Starlet Grand Hotel. Almost all of them were signed. Every dish on the menu was named for a famous movie, like the "Snow Whitefish" and the "Mystic Pizza Pie."

Sitting at the table over dinner, Lexi seemed to relax somewhat. She told us all about the training regimen, and all of the excitement leading up to the Olympics. It seemed like every major television station, magazine, and newspaper were all here—and they all wanted to talk to her. Being one of the youngest American Olympiads had its pluses. And everyone loved the story of her and Scott, or "The Olympic Power Couple," as the tabloids had taken to calling them.

"Before I forget," Lexi said over dessert, "I got these for you guys."

She pulled three small gold badges from her bag, each in the shape of the Olympic torch.

"These will get you in pretty much anywhere, so you've got free reign to check out the competitions, the backstage areas, the locker rooms, everything."

"Thanks!" we all said at the same time.

"Thank you!" said Lexi. "I feel so much better already, just knowing you're here."

There was something in her voice that made me worried. I put down my fork, the last piece of "Charlie and the Chocolate Factory Chocolate Pie" still on it.

"Has something happened?" My spidey senses were tingling.

Lexi looked around the restaurant for a moment, making sure no one was within earshot. Then she pulled something else out of her bag.

"This afternoon someone hid all these crazy snake robots in Scott's house to try and freak us out. And I found this in my locker yesterday," she half-whispered.

She handed me a long, dead rose. I unfolded the piece of paper that was tied to it. It was a photo of Lexi, ripped out of a magazine and torn in half in the process. On it had been scrawled four lines:

ROSES ARE RED,

VIOLETS ARE BLUE.

THIS ROSE IS DEAD,

SOON YOU WILL BE TOO.

CHAPTER 5

JOE

SOUND EFFECTS

It took hours for everything to calm down, even after the "snakes" were removed. After Frank, Alex Smothers, Vijay, Lexi, and her dad all left, Lee, Scott, and I began to clean the house. And this wasn't just a light dusting and vacuuming job. This was hours of work. Scott wasn't just neat—he was a total neat freak. Aunt Trudy would have loved him. By the time we were done, I thought I was going to pass out from the smell of bleach.

But finally we were alone, just Scott and I. Cleaning seemed to calm Scott down, and he was able to sit down for a little while. He brought out two glasses of raspberry seltzer water—his only "treat" while in training—and of course, two coasters to put them on. Then we got down to business.

"I need to know your schedule for the next few days—down to the minute."

"That's pretty easy," he said. "Up at five, eat and shower by five thirty, then in the gym until noon. Then it's over to the Olympic Village, either for publicity stuff, team training, or more footage for the documentary. Then I'm back here at six, dinner by seven, bed by eight."

As Scott broke down the day, I wrote it all up. It sounded like keeping track of him was going to be easy.

"And that's it?" I said.

"Well, I'll probably take a few breaks to see Lexi. And there is an Olympic gala next week that I'll have to go to. Oh, and I think Lee has me scheduled for a few nighttime press gigs. I might be hosting *Saturday Night Live* via satellite, did you hear?"

"So . . . that's your schedule, except when it isn't your schedule at all?"

"Right."

"And you're not sure exactly when any of these other things will be?"

"Right."

Maybe I had spoken too soon.

"Hey, you know what's weird?" said Scott, looking at me strangely.

"What?" I couldn't help but be excited—had he noticed something amid the snake incident that would clue us in to who had done it?

"You and that Frank guy—you look weirdly similar. I mean, if you worked at it, you could even be brothers."

I felt my stomach sink. I knew this idea of one of us going undercover was ridiculous. There was no way anyone could see the two of us and not realize Frank and I were brothers. I laughed to cover up my nervousness.

"Yeah, that's weird all right. Hey, so . . . ATAC told me that you've been getting hate mail, right? Why don't we look at that now. Maybe we'll find a clue."

I needed a change of subject, fast. Thankfully, Scott didn't seem to care. He walked out of the room and came back lugging a giant cardboard box. He gently set it on the table in front of us. It was filled to the brim with letters, postcards, and random sheets of paper.

"Wow, all of this, huh?"

"Oh, this is just the last month or two. I bring it down to a storage facility every once in a while."

"And all of it's hate mail?"

"Yep. I keep the fan mail separate. Thankfully, there's more of that then there is of this junk. This I try not to think about too much."

I couldn't believe the number of letters in the box. I pulled out a random handful. Some were typed, others handwritten, in everything from crayonlike scrawl to neat, penmanship-class perfect script. I even saw one that was the classic ransom note, made of letters cut out from magazines.

"Has it always been like this?" I asked.

"Well, I've been getting threats ever since I first started competing at the world level, when I was fifteen. But it's gotten worse since my laptop was stolen a few months ago. Whoever did it put my address and phone number up on the Internet, and ever since then, the amount of mail I've gotten has tripled. I moved and changed my number, and that made it better for a while. But last week I got this."

He reached into the box and pulled out a DVD. He turned on his giant sixty-four-inch flat screen television and slipped in the disc. There was a burst of static and then an image appeared on the screen. First it was Scott training. Then it was him sitting in a café. Then it was him in his kitchen. In his car. The images just kept coming, one after another, all eerily silent. I could tell by his haircut and the house that they were all recent. The final scene was of Scott, in his bed, asleep. The screen went black, and then a message appeared in white text. I'M WATCHING YOU. DROP OUT OF THE OLYMPICS, OR ELSE.

"After I watched that, I called you guys."

I was silent for a moment. This was some scary stuff—way worse than any hate mail could ever be, for sure. And it was my job to figure out who this sociopath was.

"Whoever did this has some pretty complete access to your life, Scott. We need to make a list of who could have gotten this footage. Who has keys to your house?"

Scott shook his head.

"Uh-uh. No way someone I knew would do this, man. These are my friends we're talking about."

"Someone did it. And whoever it was was able to get into your house while you were asleep. This is serious, Scott. We need to make a list of potential suspects."

"It's not possible!"

Scott was on his feet now, pacing. This was getting him upset, I could tell, and that was the last thing I wanted. Whoever was doing this was trying to rattle him before the Olympics, to make him lose. I needed to get the information from him and keep him calm.

"Scott, they might not know they were helping this person. Maybe their keys were stolen, or they let in someone they thought was supposed to be in the house, or something. But the list of people who have access to your house is the only starting point we have."

Scott stopped pacing.

"Okay. Well . . . there's Lee, of course. But he wants me to win more than I want me to win. And Lexi—but it isn't her, I can tell you that. That's about it, really. There was a cleaning service, but I fired them. I found I did it better myself."

He cleaned this whole house by himself, every day? He really was crazy. I thought having a maid would be, like, the best part of being rich.

I made a note to look into Lee and Lexi some more. But I had to agree with Scott, neither seemed likely.

"How about any enemies?"

Scott made a face.

"I'll take that as a yes. Who is he?"

"She. Elisa von Meter. She was my manager until last year. That's when Lee went from being my coach to being my coach *and* manager. Since then, it seems like Elisa has made her living off of doing interviews about what a terrible person I am. Now she's announced she's writing some 'tell-all' celebrity biography of me."

This sounded familiar. I felt like there was more to this story, but I couldn't remember what I had read about it. I made a note to follow up on it later.

"Why did you fire her?"

"We had some . . . personal issues, and I had to let her go last year." Scott wouldn't look me in the eye when he said it. There was definitely more to this story.

"Personal issues?"

"Yeah. You know—just, stuff."

It was clear I was going to have to do some digging into this on my own. I got her address and phone number from Scott.

"Anyone else you'd put on the enemy list?"

"Jeez . . . half the swimmers at the Olympics? I mean, no offense to them, but I'm the guy to beat. They're all after me."

"Then why only half?"

"The other half are women. They don't really care how I do." He laughed. "Look, I have to get to bed; tomorrow's a long day. There's going to be a big photo op at the Olympic Arena with all the other American athletes, and then individual press stuff. And I still have to get in all my training. So is that enough for now?"

I looked at my list. Lee, Lexi, and Elisa. Three names. It wasn't a lot to go on, but it would do for the moment.

"Sure," I said, and gathered up my stuff to head back to the hotel room ATAC had gotten me. "See you in the morning."

The Olympic Arena was an amazing building set right in the heart of downtown LA. It was really a whole complex of stadiums, pools, and tracks, all built beneath a giant glass roof. It looked sort of like a green house, except instead of a simple peaked roof, the glass ceiling here was in the shape of the Olympic torch itself.

As Scott and I walked through the main doors, heads turned. We'd already been plagued by autograph seekers for the length of the short walk from the car to the door. Now it was the professionals—journalists and paparazzi.

"Scott! Hey Scott!"

"Over here, Scott!"

"Can I ask you a few questions, Mr. Trevor?"

"Are you ready to break the record for the most Olympic gold medals won by an individual athlete?"

At that last question, Scott turned to the reporter and gave a goofy grin and a big thumbs-up. Tomorrow, that picture would be all over the newspapers.

I've always thought I was in pretty good shape. Being a superspy and all, I get a lot of exercise. But this place was filled with . . . with giants and amazons and freakishly strong-looking men and women! Often you could tell their sport just by looking at them. Legs like steel pillars? Track. Biceps bigger than my head? Discus. Doing a stretch that seemed to simultaneously dislocate their hips, neck, legs, and spine? Gymnastics.

Frank was there as well. I caught his eye and he nodded, but that was it. With Scott already a little suspicious, it seemed best not to spend too much time near him. We just went our own ways, each subtly keeping an eye on Scott. Not that I thought that anything could happen to him here, in the middle of all these people, but still—better safe than sorry.

For about an hour, all of the athletes "trained" in front of the cameras. Scott would dive in the water, swim a little ways, get a dozen or so photos taken, and then repeat the whole thing. All around the stadium, other athletes were doing the same thing, so that the papers and TV crews would have some good shots for the coming days of competition. Finally, all of the athletes changed into their official Team USA jumpsuits, which were white with red and blue piping around the wrists, necks, and ankles. Then they got together in front of the pillar that would eventually hold the Olympic torch, which was fittingly shaped like the Statue of Liberty. This was the final group photo. After this, it would be time for some real training.

"The Star-Spangled Banner" came on, and everyone in the auditorium stood with their hands over their hearts as the television cameras rolled. Suddenly, the sound cut out. There was a high-pitched feedback explosion, and then Scott's voice came rolling out of the speakers.

"This whole thing is a joke. I could whip any of those other athletes. And don't even get me started on my teammates—lazy, good-for-nothing."

For the first few seconds, people were frozen. But as Scott's voice droned on, insulting the Olympics and his team, people started gasping, laughing, and shouting. Loudest of all was Scott himself.

"What the? I never said any of that! Someone turn this off!"

Worst of all, the television cameras were all still rolling. I knew what the headlines of tomorrow's papers were going to be. This was a public relations nightmare. Even though it sounded like Scott's voice, I couldn't believe he would say all of these things. Something wasn't right, and I had to put a stop to it.

I ran to the audio booth from which the sound was being projected. There was no one in it. I looked over all the equipment. Finally, I spotted a blinking green light on what I guessed to be a CD player. I jammed the eject button, and Scott's voice finally cut out. I grabbed the CD. I wanted to take a closer look at it.

I heard someone behind me. As I turned around, a voice called out.

"Joe Hardy! I thought that was you."

CHAPTER *6*

FAKE OUT

"Whoa! Sweet ride, Nance." Joe let out a long whistle.

He was right—her car was hot! It was a pimped out sky blue convertible hybrid! I'd never seen anything like it.

"This is not standard issue," said Joe, exploring the electronics along the dashboard.

"Nope," said Nancy. "This is a specialty model. One of a kind, thanks to these two." She pointed to Bess and George.

"You guys did this?" said Joe. "I love a girl who knows her way around an engine!" He wiggled his eyebrows at Bess, and she stuck her tongue out at him.

"All right, enough flirting," I said. "Get in the back. The last thing we need is for you and I to be seen together!"

If a picture of the two of us together got out, my cover would be blown. ATAC would not like that. And there were media types all over the place. Thankfully, they'd been a bit too busy covering Scott's exit from the Olympic Arena to pay any attention to us, but still, I didn't want to take any chances. He'd shot out of there faster than I'd ever seen him go, and given his world records, that was saying a lot.

Joe jumped into the backseat between Bess and George. I took the front, next to Nancy. In a moment, we were off.

"It's good to see you!" I said, and smiled. She was just about the only girl in the world who didn't make me feel like my tongue was three times too big for my mouth.

"You too." She put her right arm around me in a quick hug.

"Nancy!" yelled Bess from the backseat.

"I see the truck! I was just saying hi to Frank. It's all good. Where are we headed?"

"We're going to take a left at the next light, get on the 405, and I'll tell you when to exit. We're heading to Moonbeam, a diner I read about on *Digg*. It's supposed to be the dive where all the Hollywood insiders go for their low-key brunches and midnight breakfasts."

"Yes!" squealed Bess. "I want to see how the stars dress on their days off!"

Once we were on the highway with the top down it was too hard to hear a word anyone said. Instead, I just stared out as the city flew by. It was nothing like Bayport. It stretched on for miles and miles. It felt like a hundred little cities, all strung together by the highway—like Christmas lights. I was happy to see Bess, George, and especially Nancy again. They were great, and always useful to have on a case. Although I was slightly worried—things seemed to get more complicated whenever they were around, and every time we had hung out, one or the other of us had nearly died.

Finally, we got to the restaurant. George was right when she called it a dive. It looked like it had seen better days . . . sometime in the 1950s. It had a giant, old-school sign that said MOONBEAM in big blinking letters. Actually, it said MOO AM, because a lot of the bulbs had burned out. But inside, it was all shiny chrome and red leather, with pictures of every celebrity to grace the silver screen in the last hundred years. There were also photos of people I didn't recognize, mostly men, who were clearly rich and important, with starlets hanging off their arms—gangsters or studio executives, it was hard to tell.

"Hi there!" said a breathy waitress as we sat down at our table. She looked like Marilyn Monroe—if Marilyn had cornrows and a septum piercing. "I'm Sugar, and I'll be your server today."

She handed us menus and sashayed back to the counter.

"Yeah," said Joe. "This place is great. Ouch!"

"Oh, I'm sorry," said Bess with a smile. "Did I kick you? My bad."

Once we ordered our food, we got down to business.

"So what are you doing here?" I asked Nancy.

"Uhhh . . . watching the Olympics?" she said with a smile.

Joe laughed. "You're a worse liar than Frank!" he said.

"All right," said Nancy. "But if I tell you why we're here, you tell us why you're here. Deal?"

I looked at Joe and nodded. It was only fair. Besides, Nancy had proven herself useful on a case more than once. And it sounded like she might already be involved in something.

Nancy pulled something out of her purse and pushed it across the table.

"Our friend Lexi Adams is one of the Olympic fencers. Her boyfriend, the swimmer Scott Trevor, has been getting death threats. And now she's started to get them too. We told her we'd come and look out for her."

"Lexi is being threatened, too? Interesting," I said.

"What do you mean, too?" asked Nancy.

"You guys are working on the Scott Trevor case, aren't you!" said George.

I nodded. "Yes—but I'm in deep cover. Even Scott doesn't know I'm with ATAC."

We gave the three of them the rundown of what ATAC had told us, and what had happened since we arrived. Our food came, and we all spent a few minutes in silence, shoveling it in.

"This is good. Really good," said Bess. She had ordered migas, which were scrambled eggs on a tortilla with salsa and a bunch of other stuff. Even just the smell was delicious.

"Good find, George," said Joe.

George smiled as she scooped up the last of her waffles.

"So, it seems like the big question is: Are Scott and Lexi the only two people being threatened, or—"

"Is it the entire American team?" I finished Nancy's sentence. "That was exactly what I was wondering."

"It seems impossible that ATAC wouldn't know the entire team was receiving death threats," said Joe.

"True—but they didn't know about the threats against Lexi, and she's Scott's girlfriend," said George.

"Right. We need someone to make some inquiries among the other American athletes. They might be afraid to come forward, so we'll have to be discreet about it," I said.

"We'll do it!" Bess grabbed George's hand and raised it up in the air with hers.

"We will?" said George.

"Yes. And we'll start with those gymnastics twins—John and Jim Ryan!"

"Ugh," said George, groaning. "She's obsessed!"

"It'll be fun. Besides, we'll get to meet a lot of famous athletes. You'll like it."

"Fine, fine."

"I want to go check in with Vijay. We should have him take a look at the CD Joe got at the arena. With all of his techie stuff, he should be able to figure out if it's real or not. Plus, I want to see if the cameras I planted in Scott's house are all up and running."

"Too bad we didn't have any in the arena," said Joe. "Or we might have gotten whoever made this CD on film!"

"Ohh," said George. "I want to go! I want to see what kind of computers ATAC has for its operatives."

"But who's going to interview the athletes with me?" asked Bess.

"I'll do it," said Nancy. "That way I can be in the arena and keep an eye on Lexi—and Scott."

"Great," said Joe. "If you guys are going to be there, I'm going to take the chance to go and talk to Scott's former manager, Elisa von Meter. Since I'm his 'personal assistant,' it makes sense that I'd be the one to go and talk to her about this tell-all book she's writing. Maybe she's trying to add a little spice to the book by threatening Scott's life."

The check arrived, and I scooped it up.

"One of the perks of working for ATAC," I said. "They pay for all the food."

On her way back to the Olympic Arena, Nancy dropped George, Joe, and me at the hotel where Vijay was staying. Joe grabbed a cab, while George and I took in Vijay's fancy digs. The hotel was one of those huge ultramodern buildings, all glass and chrome. It rose like a shiny steel needle up above the city, higher than any of the surrounding buildings.

"Yes?" said the clerk, in that way that was perfectly polite, yet still somehow managed to convey that he felt that we two *children* should not be here unescorted.

"Frank Hardy here to see Vijay Patel," I told him.

"Oh, yes," he smiled, his manner suddenly changing. "Allow me to call Mr. Patel."

There was a quiet phone exchange, and then he turned back to us.

"Go right up. The last elevator on the left goes directly to the penthouse suite."

As we walked away, George whispered to me.

"Did he say 'penthouse'? What gives?"

I shrugged my shoulders. I hadn't seen Vijay's hotel room yet.

The last elevator turned out to be a clear glass box finished in brass that went up the outside of the hotel, giving us an incredible view of the city.

"Wow!" was all George or I could say.

The elevator opened up directly into his apartment. It was like a giant greenhouse floating above LA. It felt like you were outside, only without the wind or smog or rain. Plus, there were some real comfortable couches and a ton of audio equipment, computer monitors, and televisions.

"How come you got the sweet digs?" I asked. "This place is off the hook!"

"Necessary," Vijay said. "With all the smog in this city, I need a line of sight on both the Olympic Arena and Scott's house if the transmissions are going to come through clear. This is the only place in all of LA that met my requirements. Oh, and you should check out the private garden up above. It's suh-weet!"

"This setup is incredible!" George was looking at the computers. "You've got live feeds coming in from nine different cameras. And is that a gait recognition set up?"

"Yup. So it can alert me whenever Scott is onscreen, or whenever a new person it hasn't seen before is in Scott's house."

"What's gait recognition?" I asked. It was a rare moment when I was the least geeky person in the room.

"It's software that tries to recognize people by how they walk," said Vijay.

"I heard it's pretty easy to throw off," said George.

"Yeah—you can't depend on it, but it can be helpful."

Vijay had got a pretty good view of almost every room in Scott's house. Ditto the arena, though there were a few blind spots there—the place was just too big to blanket it with recorders. And some areas we couldn't get into, like the women's lockers rooms. Otherwise, we totally could have seen who slipped the note into Lexi's locker.

"What's with the static?" I asked. A few of the screens were fuzzy, or had lines running through them.

"There's a little signal interference—buildings or smog or television transmissions, I don't know. This was the best I could get. Anyway. You didn't just come here to check out my sweet pad, so whatcha got for me?"

I dropped the disk into his hands and explained the situation.

"Intriguing," Vijay said. "Maybe Scott isn't the good little athlete he seems like?"

"I think someone faked the recording, but I can't be sure."

"Let's check it out!"

Vijay popped the CD into one of his computers. Scott's voice began booming through the apartment. It was so loud it was almost painful.

"Sorry!" Vijay said, as he hurried to turn the sound down. "I was listening to some ragga earlier—it always helps me when I'm coding."

He listened to Scott's voice for a second.

"Sounds legit," he said. "But let's find out."

Vijay pulled up a new program that broke the sound file into waves.

"Total fake," he said.

"How can you tell?" I asked.

"See here?" Vijay pointed to the screen. "This wave represents Scott's voice. See how it's all broken up and choppy, not smooth? That means it was pieced together from a whole bunch of other recordings. Someone created this sentence, using words Scott had actually spoken, but stitching them together to make a whole new sentence."

George let out a low whistle. "Whoever did this has some pretty sophisticated tech!"

Vijay nodded. "This is not your hobbyist's setup. This is the real deal.

"I wonder . . . ," said Vijay. He hopped up and started rummaging through a pile of discs. He selected one and popped it into another laptop.

"Yep!" he said, triumphantly.

"What?" asked George, excited.

"This CD is a threatening video that was sent to Scott. It's all footage of him in various places."

"Right," I said. "Joe told us about that."

"Well, if you compare the files, it looks like these discs were made using the same computer programs. I think Scott's angered some geek, somewhere."

"That would go along with the robotic snakes," I murmured. Now we were getting somewhere!

George's phone gave a quick beep, the sound of a text message coming in. She fished it out of her pocket.

"Oh no!" she yelled.

"What?" I asked.

"Look!"

George passed the phone to me. The screen read:

@ hospital w/ Lexi.

CHAPTER 7

JOE

INTERVIEWING THE ENEMY

After Nancy dropped me off, I went to flag down a taxi. But after Nancy's sweet ride, the idea of being stuck in a smelly, dirty taxi seemed horrible. Luckily, right at that moment one of the big double-decker tourist buses swung by. I'd always wanted to ride on the top of one, and I figured it would help me learn the layout of the city, which could be useful if, like, we ended up in a car chase or something. You never know what might happen when you're a superspy.

"LA History and Mystery Tour! Get on in," said the driver.

"Are you going to—"

"We go everywhere there is to go in this city. City of Angels, City of Demons. You don't want to miss this, kid."

I got in. I figured I could use the GPS on my phone to tell me when we were close to Elisa's house, and I could hop out then. Besides, I was only going to be in LA once, so I needed to make the most of it! And since Frank was getting to hang out with George, I deserved to have some fun too.

Looking out over the city, it was easy to see why so many people were drawn to LA. There were models everywhere! Or at least, people who looked like models. In a city full of stars and wannabe stars, it was hard to tell the difference. But despite the smog and the dirt, LA did seem to have a feeling of excitement and money and adventure. Anyone, it seemed, could be the next big thing, even the guy on the corner selling gyros and schwarma from a cart.

The driver talked like a ringleader at a circus, a real showman. He rattled off stories and facts left and right. Maybe *he* would be the next big thing.

"And right here, folks, right here on this very street, right outside Grauman's Chinese Theatre, is the Hollywood Walk of Fame. Here we have the footprints, handprints, and sometimes cigar prints of some of Hollywood's biggest legends, from Groucho Marx and Joan Crawford to Jim Carrey and Emma Watson. They say you don't know a person until you've walked a mile in their shoes—well, here you can walk a mile in the footprints of the stars!"

I was only half-listening to him, however. I spent most of the time doing some research on my phone. Elisa, it turns out, had been a PR professional before she had become Scott's manager. She'd actually started her own high-profile celebrity agency, which she'd closed to work for Scott. It was her work that had made Scott the household name that he'd become. And a little more than a year later, he'd fired her. No wonder she was PO'd. And boy, did she show it. The tabloids from the time were filled with screaming matches between the two of them. She'd threatened him repeatedly—and even slashed his tires one night!

Since then, she'd put a lot of her time—and her PR connections—into smearing his name. A little more searching brought up a series of tell-all interviews about him on a celebrity blog called *Stalker*. It looked like Scott wasn't the only one she was gossiping about. In some of the interviews, she'd branched out to dishing the dirt on other big athletes she'd met during her time with him. Including Lexi, who she called both "uptight" and "stupid." It seemed her main project now was shopping around an unauthorized biography of Scott, entitled *Waterlogged: My Life with the Selfish Teenager Who Became America's Darling*. She'd also released some "secret footage" of Scott to the media. Most of it was *America's Funniest Home Videos* type of stuff: him messing up, tripping into the pool, hitting his head while swimming, etc. But at least one of the tapes was of him having a total melt-down because his training area was a mess. It definitely made him look bad—and crazy. Like the tape that was played at the reception earlier. And given her PR and Internet savvy, it wouldn't be surprising if she knew her way around tech stuff.

Finally, my phone beeped to let me know that we were near Elisa's house, in a neighborhood known as Silver Lake. It was one of the supertrendy, hip areas of the city. There were people in tight jeans and big sunglasses everywhere, with hair that reminded me of the biker gang we'd faced last week. I didn't find a lake anywhere, but I did see quite a few pools. I could get used to this city, I decided. I hopped out and headed to the address ATAC had given me, taking notes on Elisa the whole way.

Suspect Profile

Name: Elisa von Meter

Hometown: Los Angeles, California

Occupation: Professional gossip

Physical description: Five-six; long, curly red hair; heart-shaped face; athletic. In a city of models, she holds her own on the pretty scale.

Suspected of: Sending death threats to Scott Trevor. Filming him in his sleep. Sabotaging his public appearances. And maybe, now, going after Lexi, too.

Motive: Everyone wants to see the golden boy fail—and then read about it after. Scott losing at the Olympics could be the best possible ending for her new book.

Suspicious behavior: She's already shown that she'd been filming Scott in secret all along. She's threatened him in public before. Maybe now she's upping the ante.

I let out a low whistle. She sounded like a real piece of work. This was going to be a tough interview. I mentally psyched myself up as I walked along the path to her little corner bungalow. It was classic California style: two small palm trees out front, red tile roof, large garden in the back.

I barely had a chance to knock on the door before it was flung open—but only about two inches. One fierce green eye peaked out through below the safety chain.

"What? I don't want any."

The door started to close.

"Ms. von Meter?" I yelled.

The door paused. Then I heard a quick intake of breath. The door shut the rest of the way.

"Darn," I said. This was going to be tough.

Then, to my surprise, the door opened the rest of the way. Behind it stood Lexi.

Or, no, not Lexi—just a woman who looked a lot like her. Same hair, same build, same heart-shaped face. But this woman's green eyes were in constant, angry motion, as though she were scanning the horizon for an attack.

"You," she said. "You're his new personal assistant. Joe . . ."

She pulled a small spiral-bound notebook from her back pocket and flipped to a page, seemingly at random. "Hardy. Joe Hardy. I've been wanting to talk to you."

She gave me a smile that was meant, I thought, to be friendly. Instead, it was the kind of smile a wolf gave a rabbit.

"Come in."

She put her hand on my arm and virtually yanked me inside. Maybe this wasn't going to be as hard as I thought.

She half-guided, half-threw me down on a couch in her living room. Before I could get a word in edgewise, Elisa had pulled a tape recorder out of another of her pockets.

"It's August Fourth, 2010. The time is four p.m. This is Elisa von Meter interviewing Joe Hardy, personal assistant to one Scott Trevor. Location of interview is my living room."

Seems like Elisa wanted to interview me as much as I wanted to interview her. Maybe I could use this to my advantage.

"So, Mr. Hardy, what's it like working for the notoriously OCD Scott Trevor? Unpleasant? Horrible? Or just merely painful?

She waited expectantly, her digital recorder pointing directly at my face. Thank God she had a digital recorder, I thought, as I slipped my hand into my pocket and punched a quick activation code into my special ATAC-issued phone. This trick wouldn't work on an old-school tape recorder, but the activation code I had just keyed in would scramble any file a digital recorder tried to create. We were officially "off the record." But there was no point in telling Elisa that—not yet, anyway. It was time to bargain.

"I won't talk on tape," I said.

"Joe—can I call you Joe? Let's be reasonable. You came here because you want something from me. I want something from you. I see no reason why we can't help each other out. I can even give you a pseudonym for the book."

I pretended to think about it. "Promise you won't use my real name?"

"Of course."

"Okay," I said. "Scott's pretty tough to work for. He's constantly asking me to clean and move things around. Everything has to be just perfect or he goes totally crazy on me."

Elisa cackled and did a little dance in her seat. She was eating this up.

"That's actually kind of why I came to see you."

"Tell me more," she said.

"Well, it's just—how did you deal with it? I mean, most of the time, it's okay, but recently, with all the threats he's been getting, he's just gotten more and more crazy." I wanted her to tip her hand. If I could get her talking about the threats, maybe she'd let something slip. At least I'd be able to tell if she knew something, even if I couldn't get her to reveal it.

"There have been more threats?" she said. She sounded upset.

I nodded.

"This is not good, Joe. Scott has got to be in peak condition. This is the most important week of his life. You've got to help him get through this." She was on her feet now, pacing. "Scott has never been able to deal with stress well. Really drives him crazy—he'll stop sleeping. Watch out for that. Make sure he sleeps. Got it? Make sure."

This was not the reaction I expected. It was almost like she was . . . *helping* me.

"But don't you want Scott to lose?"

She let out a single bark of a laugh.

"What, are you kidding me? He is my cash cow. If he wins at the Olympics, if he breaks the record for most gold medals by a single athlete, my book is golden. I'm set. Everyone wants to hear the juicy gossip behind the scenes of the winner. But no one buys books about losers."

She had a point. She might be mean and amoral, but when it came to this, her best interest was Scott's best interest.

"But what about all that secret footage of him you released? Wasn't that going to throw him off his game too?"

"That? That was months ago. I was angry then. Besides, that was right when he dumped me for that little tramp he's with now."

Dumped her? That was something Scott hadn't mentioned. He'd been shifty about exactly why he'd let Elisa go, but this might explain a few things.

"Now, I'm thinking clearly. Besides, that was just to show him I was serious. And it wasn't even my idea in the first pla—"

She seemed to catch herself. *Darn*, I thought, *just as things were about to get interesting.* She laughed again, a more human sound this time.

"Oops. Don't need to have that on tape."

She hit the back button, probably intending to tape over the last few seconds of the conversation. But when she hit play to find her place, all that came out was static. I had a feeling my interview was about to be over.

"What the heck?" she said. Even though I wished I could get more information out of her, I couldn't keep a smile from playing across my lips. Elisa noticed.

"You did this, didn't you? You're jamming my recorder. You smarmy little brat."

For all that she was much shorter than me, Elisa towered above me on the couch, five-feet-six-inches of pure fury. I couldn't help but laugh.

"Sorry about that, Elisa. But you've been real helpful." I stood up and started to walk to the door.

"Get out of my house!" she screamed at my back.

"You're the best," I yelled over my shoulder. "Let's do lunch! Have your people call my people!" I swung the door shut behind me. A second later, something exploded against the back of it. Judging from the sound of the impact, it was her digital recorder.

Unless she was the world's best actress, Elisa didn't seem to be behind the death threats. But she did know how to use recorders and other technical equipment, which still kept her in the running in my mind. Maybe she was working with someone else—after all, she'd mentioned the secret footage not being her idea. I needed to get more information from her, but after that episode, there was no way she was going to talk to me again.

Maybe Nancy could talk to her? Woman to woman? I didn't know quite how that sort of thing worked— I imagined there were sleepovers and hair-braiding involved. But if it worked, I was ready to ask Nancy to try it.

My phone buzzed. Speaking of Nancy, it was a text message from her:

"@ hospital w/ Lexi."

A sick feeling welled up in my stomach, as though I'd just been punched. I started to jog along the road. I just hoped this neighborhood had taxis . . .

CHAPTER

NANCY

MAKING THE CUT

"Well, that was quite the surprise!"

Bess still couldn't get over running into Joe and Frank here in LA. It was all she could talk about since we'd dropped them off.

"I mean, it's like you can't leave River Heights without running into them. They are, like, everywhere. Not that I'm complaining. They're both so cute! And so funny. And—"

"And so on a case, remember? Just like we are."

"Yeah. The case of the supercute brothers!"

I had to laugh at that. She was right, the Hardys were a great pair. And it was exciting to be working on a case with them again. I tried not to think about how the last time we all hung out, we also all almost died. In fact, pretty much every time I saw Frank and Joe, I ended up dangling from something or with a gun pointed at my head. They sure knew how to party.

After I'd found Joe by the sound equipment, I'd told Lexi that we were going to go "catch up with some old friends." I didn't want to mention ATAC to her. They tried to keep that a secret. Besides, she'd been too busy calming down Scott to pay much attention to me. I told her we'd meet up with her in a few hours. I figured we still had some time to talk to some of the athletes before we went looking for her.

By the time we got back to the Olympic Arena, almost all of the journalists were gone. The main competition area was closed, and the athletes were all training in the various sub-complexes. We pinned on the passes that Lexi had given us—little Olympic-torch-shaped badges. They worked like magic. There was nowhere, it seemed, where we weren't allowed to go.

We passed a group of American athletes, easily picked out by their red, white, and blue tracksuits, and Bess tried to make conversation.

"Hi there!" she said, her smile beaming.

There were a few nods, but most of the athletes just kept talking to one another.

"My wind sprints are totally lagging today. My coach is going to kill me."

"I hear you. That guy from Ghana was right behind

me on the one hundred meter. I've got to cut one-tenth off my time before the games start."

I noticed one woman standing slightly off by herself, and tried to talk to her.

"So, what do you play?"

"Play?" She looked at me as though I'd asked her to massage my feet.

"Yeah, like, what sport do you play?"

"This is the Olympics. We're the top athletes *in the world*. We don't 'play' at anything. We compete. I run relays."

"Oh, well. That's nice," I mumbled. The woman walked away from me with a snort. I didn't even get her name. I spotted Bess standing by herself a few feet away and hurried over to join her, my cheeks burning.

"This might be harder than I thought," Bess said.

"Yeah. I think I just insulted someone."

"That's better than I've done—no one will even talk to me!"

"Even if they did, how do you work 'are you being threatened?' into a casual conversation?"

"We need some sort of gimmick."

We stood there thinking for a few minutes. I stared out across the auditorium. A few hundred feet away, a journalist was interviewing the same woman I had just spoken to. She was talking and laughing. How did they do it?

Then it came to me.

"We'll tell them we're journalists! And we're doing a report on jealousy among star athletes. That way, we've got a reason to talk to them."

"Great idea!" Bess pulled a small notebook out of her pocket. "This way, I can even take notes without looking suspicious."

With our new plan, we began to work the room. A few of the athletes still wouldn't talk to us, but many of them seemed eager to talk to the press. It made sense. The more publicity they got, the more likely they were to get sponsorship deals, and that's where the real money was. They might have competed for the love of the sport, but they had to make money somehow.

Very quickly, though, we ran into a new problem: Nearly everyone had a story of being threatened or getting hate mail. Like Lexi had said, it was part of the life of any public figure. Most of them thought it was pretty funny. A few seemed upset that people would spend that much time thinking terrible things about people they didn't even know. But no one seemed particularly upset or scared or freaked out when we asked.

We worked our way slowly around the training facility. Suddenly, Bess grabbed my arm and squealed.

"Look! It's the Ryan twins." She pointed to two dark-haired, powerfully built guys off to our right. Both were classically handsome, with piercing eyes and warm, smiling faces. "I'm totally going to inter-view them."

I watched as she ran over to them. Even at a dis-tance, I could see them smiling at her. It looked like her dream was finally coming true.

With Bess off interviewing the Ryan twins, I looked around for another athlete to talk to. Near me, one of the female swimmers was toweling off.

"Hi there! I'm Nancy." I held out my hand.

"Isabelle Helene," she said. She grabbed my hand in hers. She had a powerful handshake. She was a good four inches taller than I was. She was one of the older athletes in the room, probably in her early thirties. She had a regal look to her, one part beautiful, one part proud. As she pulled off her swim cap, her long, chest-nut brown hair tumbled down her shoulders.

"I'm doing an article for *Sporting Monthly*," I began saying. I had no idea if there really was a *Sporting Monthly* magazine, but there were so many journal-ists crawling around I figured no one else would know either. "We're looking into jealousy in the world of high-powered athletes."

Isabelle's mouth twisted into a tight grimace.

"What are you insinuating? You journalists and your rumormongering. I have nothing to say."

She turned away from me sharply and strode off. She wasn't the first athlete to give us the cold shoulder, but she was definitely one of the rudest. I hoped she slipped in her own puddles!

Bess bounced back over a few minutes later, eager to tell me everything the Ryan twins had said to her, including their favorite colors, foods, and places to travel.

"Any threats or anything?"

"A few obsessive fans—not me—but nothing like what Lexi and Scott have been experiencing. You get anything from that woman?"

"Just a whole lot of attitude. But it seems pretty clear that whatever is going on, they're targeting Lexi and Scott specifically."

"Yeah. Speaking of which, it looks like Lexi is about to have a practice match. Want to go watch?"

Bess pointed across the gym, where Lexi was getting into her fencing suit. I hesitated for a moment. It didn't seem like anyone else was being threatened, but we hadn't talked to *all* of the athletes yet, so we couldn't know for sure. But I was curious to see Lexi fence with another person at her skill level, someone who could give her a real run for her money.

"Sure, let's check it out."

Lexi fenced with the saber, which is one of the three blades used in modern fencing—the others being the foil and the epee. Saber is the one that's most like the sword fighting you see in movies. You can strike with the edge of the blade, as well as the point. It's what Lexi was teaching me, since it was the most likely to come in handy if I ever got in a sword fight, which given my life, isn't as unlikely as it sounds.

"Fencing, as a sport, has quite the prestigious history," I whispered to Bess as Lexi and her opponent suited up. "The first recorded use of the term 'fence' is in William Shakespeare's *Merry Wives of Windsor*. It is one of only four sports to be in every modern Olympics."

The small audience that had gathered around the fencing mats grew quiet as the two women took their places. The starting pose of fencing looked almost like ballet: one leg back, foot pointing to the side, the front arm raised, weapon ready.

"En *garde!*" yelled one of the coaches.

For a moment, no one moved. No one even seemed to breathe. Then it began. The two fencers were lunging at each other, twisting, slashing, stabbing. The blades flickered so fast they were nearly invisible. The sharp sound of metal-on-metal echoed throughout the arena. They danced back and forth across the mats rapidly. At first, Lexi was being forced back toward the edge of the mats, which was dangerous, because stepping off the mats could make you lose. But she quickly recovered, and drove her opponent backward.

Step by step, Lexi seemed to be winning. Her opponent was definitely on the defensive. In a few seconds, it seemed Lexi would make the first point of the game, by striking her opponent with either the point or the edge of the blade—saber fencing allowed you to do either.

But suddenly her opponent made a risky move, a full-out lunge, throwing herself directly at Lexi. If she missed, or if Lexi parried her blade, she would be left entirely open and be unable to defend herself. But she didn't miss. The point of her saber got Lexi in the leg.

And Lexi screamed. Not a sound of surprise or frustration, but one of pain. As I watched dumbfounded, blood blossomed on her all-white fencing costume. Something had gone horribly wrong.

"Lexi!" I yelled. Bess and I stood up and ran toward her side. Her opponent was standing there in total shock, not moving, her blade still sticking in Lexi's leg. In fact, no one seemed to be moving. Everyone was so surprised.

Everyone except Lexi's dad, who beat us to her side. She was on the ground now, clutching her leg, moaning in pain. But instead of helping her, Lexi's dad turned on the teammate who had been her opponent.

"What did you do? How could you be so stupid!" He was screaming at her, as though she had done this on purpose. Even with what little fencing experience I had, I knew that with a proper fencing sword, there was no way you could break the skin, no matter how hard you lunged. Someone had tampered with the equipment.

"I'm sorry, I'm so sorry. Oh, God. Is she okay?" The

girl had taken off her mask, and was apologizing in between sobs.

I knelt down by Lexi's side.

"Lexi, listen to me. I have some first aid training. Is it okay if I look at the wound?"

Lexi nodded, her face pale. She'd bitten down on her lower lip to keep herself from moaning.

"Bess, give me my bag, and go find a doctor." They had to have one on call for emergencies. In fact, why weren't they here already? This was feeling more and more suspicious by the second.

Bess handed me my bag and took off at a run. I opened the bag and pulled out my handy little medic kit. I pulled on a pair of latex gloves, to keep from getting blood on my skin or any germs from my hands in the wound.

"The puncture is small," I said half to Lexi and half to myself. "But it's deep. I think it's going to need stitches. Here's what we're going to do."

I fished a tiny pair of shears out of my medic kit.

"I don't want to remove the sword, because you'll bleed more. But I'm going to cut it, so we can move you without it pulling or getting caught on things. This might hurt a little. Take my hand, and squeeze as hard as you need to. Ready?"

I cut the sword about an inch away from where it entered Lexi's leg. Then I had someone hand me a bottle of water and a cup. I poured clean water over the wound to wash it and placed gauze around the tiny remains of the sword to stabilize it. Finally, I taped the cup over it, so that nothing would touch it while we moved Lexi.

Suddenly, Bess was at my side.

"The doctor is busy with some sort of emergency at the pool. He'll be here as soon as he can."

I felt my jaw set in anger. That wasn't good enough.

"Well, then we're just going to have to take her to the hospital ourselves," I said, through gritted teeth. "And the police."

"No!"

This was the first word Lexi had spoken since she'd been stabbed.

"Are you all right?" I looked down to see if I had missed anything, if something was still hurting her.

"We can't go to the police. My dad . . ." Her eyes cut over to where her father stood, still screaming at her teammate. "If he found out about the threats, he'd . . . I don't even know what he would do. Please, just say it was an accident. You can figure this out, Nancy, I know you can."

I hesitated. She had every right to keep this a secret, but I worried that it might put her in even greater danger. Maybe I couldn't tell her father, or the police—but there were two people who needed to know. With one arm under her shoulder to help Lexi stand, I pulled out my cell phone and texted Joe and Frank.

CHAPTER 9

FRANK

TWO KILLERS FOR THE PRICE OF ONE?

"We're nearly there!" George yelled to me as we raced through the streets of downtown LA. She had her smart phone out and was reading the directions to the Good Samaritan Hospital from the screen. "Take a left at the next corner." It wasn't that far away, and given LA's traffic, we figured we'd make better time on foot.

We arrived, out of breath, outside of the wide white expanse of the hospital, just as a taxi pulled in.

"Wait for me!" Joe yelled. He threw some money at the cabbie, and together we all ran into the lobby. We nearly flew up the steps to Lexi's room.

Lexi lay on the bed, her eyes half-closed. Between the exhaustion and the painkillers they had her on, she wasn't fully conscious. There was a bandage wrapped around her left leg, but she didn't look too bad. Nancy and Bess were sitting in two chairs on either side of the room, half comforting Lexi, half guarding her. A curtain ran down the middle of the room, cutting it in two.

"Poor Lexi!" George murmured.

"What's going on?" Lexi mumbled, her eyes still closed.

"Gang's all here," said Nancy. "It's a party." She stood up and stepped away from the bed. In a hushed voice, she explained what had happened.

"How is she?" I asked when Nancy was done.

"She'll be all right. The wound wasn't too deep. The doctors said she needs to take tomorrow off, but she can go back to training after that. But take a look at this."

Nancy pulled a plastic sandwich bag out of her pocket. Inside was a small piece of metal.

"The doctors let me keep it. It's the tip of the saber Lexi's opponent was wielding."

She passed it around to us.

"What about it?" I asked. Clearly, it was the tip of the sword that had injured Lexi, but I wasn't sure what I was supposed to see in it.

"Whoever did this was smart. I looked at the rest of the sword while I was giving Lexi first aid. They hadn't tampered with most of it—if they'd sharpened the edge or anything, an experienced fencer would have noticed the weight difference. All they did was sharpen the point the tiniest bit. Not enough so that you'd feel the difference if you were just holding it—"

"But enough to make it dangerous," Joe finished.

"Not just dangerous," Nancy replied. "Lethal. If that strike had been in her chest, the doctors said it could have punctured a lung."

A commotion had begun in the hall while Nancy was talking. It got louder and louder, until soon, a recognizable voice was screaming outside of the door.

"I don't care who you are! She's my daughter, and I am going to see her!"

David Adams shoved the door so hard it slammed into the wall. An gray-haired nurse with a stern face trailed after him.

"Sir, your daughter needs rest! And you are being belligerent."

"You don't know what my daughter needs! You incompetents! If she can't compete tomorrow, I will sue you!"

"Dad?"

Lexi's voice drifted up weakly from the bed. Mr. Adams shot the nurse one last dirty look, and then rushed to her side.

"Hey sweetie, don't worry. Daddy's here. It's going to be okay. We'll have you back in training in no time."

"My leg hurts."

"You were injured by that stupid teammate of yours.

I handled her. But you've got to be more careful, sweetheart. The Olympics are only days away. You need to be in top form. This is what you've been training up to for years."

"It was an accident, Dad. It wasn't her fault."

"Well, it was someone's fault! And I plan on finding out whose. They'll be hearing from our lawyers."

"Lexi!"

Everyone turned as Scott rushed through the door. His manager, Lee, followed closed behind. Scott was out of breath, and from the redness around his eyes, it looked as though he'd been crying. I slipped quickly behind the curtain that separated Lexi's half of the room from the other half. Luckily, she didn't have a roommate. I couldn't be spotted here—this deep cover thing was difficult!

"Scott!" A smile spread on Lexi's face, and she held her hand out toward him.

"Are you all right? No one could tell me what happened. There was an accident in the pool—Isabelle slipped and hit her head, and the doctor and I were trying to help her—and then next thing I knew people were telling me you'd been rushed to the hospital."

He rushed toward her bedside, but Mr. Adams got between them.

"You!" His voice had returned to its usual four million decibels. He put his hand on Scott's shoulder and shoved him backward. "I'm sure this is your fault. If Lexi wasn't so busy mooning over you, that girl would never have gotten through her guard, and she wouldn't be here, in the hospital, bleeding!"

From behind the curtain, I watched as Nancy and Joe ran over and grabbed Mr. Adams from either side. He looked like he was about to punch Scott in the face!

"Dad, calm down! This isn't Scott's fault!"

"Yes it is! He's been nothing but trouble since you two met! It's his fault you finished third in the women's World Championships—keeping you up all night on the telephone, distracting you from your training."

As David ranted and raved, the door to the hospital room opened. I tried to signal to Joe, but I couldn't get his attention. A camera peeped in through the gap in the door. The press! This was the last thing Scott needed. But I couldn't do anything from where I was.

Nancy tried to calm Mr. Adams down, but he ignored her. The door opened wider, and I saw a whole pack of reporters outside—Alex Smothers, a blond woman I recognized from ESPN, and a number of others. I groaned inside. This was turning into a disaster. Luckily, Lee was paying attention.

"No photographs, please," he said firmly. He stepped out of the room, making sure to block the view of the cameras as he did so, and shut the door firmly behind him.

"He's the worst thing that ever happened to you, Lexi!" Mr. Adams was still yelling. "He's ruining your life! He should just go away."

Ruining your life? Just go away? Those sounded like threats to me . . .

Suspect Profile

Name: David Adams

Hometown: River Heights, same as Nancy

Occupation: Manager/overbearing father

Physical description: Five-nine, barrel-chested, with a long beard and biceps the size of my head. Before he quit to become Lexi's full-time manager, he'd been a carpenter, and he has the powerful muscles to show for it.

Suspected of: Possibly wanting to kill Scott Trevor. Scratch that— he definitely wants to kill him. But is he willing to do it? That's the question.

Motive: Scott and Lexi had been dating for almost a year, and Mr. Adams blames Scott for distracting Lexi from her training, and for getting injured.

Suspicious behavior: Mr. Adams's temper is explosive. And now his threats against Scott have been captured on camera.

Of course, Mr. Adams would never threaten Lexi— that was obvious after seeing them together for only five minutes. She was his world. So were we dealing with two psychopaths? I wished I'd had a chance to find out if Joe had learned anything from Elisa.

The door to the hospital room burst all the way open. I was expecting more press to shove in, but it was hospital security—three big guys in blue uniforms. Apparently, all of the yelling had attracted some attention.

"Excuse me, sir, you're going to have to come with us."

"Like heck I am! This is my daughter and I'm not going anywhere."

"Sir, I do not want to have to Taser you, but I will."

"I will sue every person in this hospital! I oughta—"

"Dad. It's okay. I'm feeling better. I'll leave with you." Lexi had dragged herself up to a sitting position. Nancy rushed over to her side.

"Are you sure about this?"

Lexi nodded her head. "Yes. I'm feeling better already. And it's easier this way."

Mr. Adams put one of Lexi's arms around his shoulder and helped her stand. Together, they left the room.

"Lexi, call me!" Scott said as she passed by.

"Don't you talk to her," growled Mr. Adams. Lexi met his eyes over her father's shoulder and nodded almost imperceptibly. Something told me that despite Mr. Adams's overbearing ways, he wasn't going to control his daughter that easily.

Once they left, Scott seemed to realize who else was in the room. He quickly shut the door, blocking the view of the cameras that were still in the hallway. Since the shouting seemed to be over, most of them had left to film Lexi painfully making her way down the hall.

"What are you doing here?" Scott asked Joe.

"Uh . . . I, uh, saw Lexi get hurt, and since you weren't around, I followed her to the hospital to make sure she was okay."

Scott knew about ATAC, but there was no point in letting Scott know that Nancy knew. She wasn't supposed to, but she had figured it all out the first time we'd met, and since then, she had proven herself to be very useful on many cases. Still, since we were supposed to be secret agents and all, we tried not to let the word out.

"And my name's Nancy. I'm from Lexi's hometown."

"Oh, right—Nancy Drew. She told me you were coming. And this must be Bess and George. Lexi's told me all about you girls." A smile spread across Scott's face. Even though he was exhausted, stressed out, and scared, he still knew how to charm an audience. "I'm glad she's got some old friends out here to support her."

"We're doing everything we can, Scott." Nancy put her hand on Scott's arm.

"You don't know the half of it," George mumbled. Nancy kicked her in the shin.

"What was that?" Scott said to George.

"Nothing . . . I, uh, was just wondering how you stay so fit."

Scott launched into a description of his workout routine, and George did her best to look interested. I wished he would leave so I could come out. Finally, Lee reappeared.

"I think they're gone now," he said. "Scott, we should leave before any of them try to come back and get a comment from you."

"Right. Right. Joe, can we give you a ride?"

Joe slipped his arm around Bess's shoulder.

"Actually, I promised these lovely ladies I'd give them a quick tour of the city. Unless you need me?" I could tell Joe wanted to share the information he had gained. But his first priority was to help Scott, in any way necessary.

Scott was fooled by the act, though. He got a small smile on his face.

"No, that's all right. You have fun tonight. We'll talk in the morning."

He gave Joe a friendly punch on the shoulder, and then he and Lee left.

"Phew," I said, stepping out from behind the curtain. "That was close."

"Yeah," Joe said. "Let's get out of here before he comes back for something."

The five of us piled into Nancy's car and headed back to her hotel room. I was in the front with Nancy, and Joe squeezed into the back between Bess and George.

On the way, we took turns filling one another in on what we had learned.

"So whoever this is, they're targeting Lexi and Scott specifically," I said, once we were done talking.

"Right. And I don't think Mr. Adams would ever hurt Lexi—he's just got a temper," said Nancy.

"I think Elisa would hurt anyone she had to, if it made a good story. But she had a pretty good reason not to hurt Scott. And a really good one to hate Lexi," chimed in Joe.

"So are we dealing with two separate cases? Or are we missing something else entirely?" I said.

No one answered.

CHAPTER 10

JOE

SHOCK TO THE SYSTEM

Suspects in this case were beginning to pile up, but try as I might, I couldn't make any of them match with everything that was happening. Some piece of the puzzle was missing, and I just hoped we found it before someone ended up seriously injured. For the time being, I did the only thing I could think of: I stuck to Scott like gum to the sole of a shoe. I wanted to ask him about what Elisa had said about their relationship, but I never got a chance to talk to him alone.

"Heads up! Coming through."

The Olympic Arena was full of people moving things, setting up stands and equipment, training, and taking photos. Just walking from the door to the pool area was like running an obstacle course. And I mean running—Scott's slowest pace seemed to be a jog. When he really wanted to get somewhere in a hurry, I bet he could have taken on some of the sprinters in the arena.

"So, I'll need you to call my massage therapist. We're pushing back training tonight by another hour, so he'll have to be at the house at eight thirty, not seven thirty. Oh, and tell whoever it is that you have delivering dinner that I don't like onions. I could barely eat whatever that was yesterday."

"Uh. Got it. Yeah. Massage. Onions."

Did I mention that the entire time we were jogging through the arena, he kept up a steady monologue of things that needed to get done? And that he seemed to have forgotten that my cover story as his personal assistant was just that—a cover story? Oh well. The life of an ATAC agent: so glamorous.

Once we made it poolside, things calmed down. Scott's focus narrowed down to just the water, and any things he had for me to do were forgotten. While he warmed up and greeted his teammates, I chatted with Lee. My gut said he was innocent, but I thought I would check in on him anyway.

"So how did you end up coaching?" I asked as we watched Scott swim his first trial heat. We were sitting on the bleachers nearby, and Lee had an old-school stopwatch in his hand. It was hardly the sort of fancy digital tech that our stalker seemed to enjoy, but maybe it was just to throw us off.

"Oh, I used to be a swimmer myself," he replied. "'Course, then I got this, and that all changed."

He slapped his leg, and I heard a hollow sound.

"What do you mean?"

He pulled up his right pant leg. Beneath it was a prosthetic limb.

"I was in a car accident. A pretty bad one. I was lucky just to lose one leg. It kept me out of the pool for a long time. At first I couldn't swim, and then I didn't want to. Everything that reminded me of my life before the accident just made me angry. But after a few years, I found I missed it. So I started coaching a local swim team, and that's how I met Scott. We've been working together ever since."

That didn't sound much like the motivation of a crazy stalker. In fact, whenever Lee talked about Scott, he sounded more like a proud father than anything else. I was about to ask him a few more questions, when a voice called out to us.

"Perfect! That was perfect. Joe—we don't have a signed release form from you yet, do we? Of course, I could just use the audio from that, but I think the actual footage of the two of you sitting and talking is great, too. Here, Joe, sign this and we'll put you on TV."

Alex Smothers was standing there with his camera

in hand. And it sounded like he'd taped our entire conversation. He was waving some form in my face.

"I don't think—" I started to say something, and Alex pointed his camera right in my face.

"Wait—hold that thought. Let me just get you in focus."

"No. I don't want to be on camera."

"Shy? Don't worry. You've got a great face. The audience will love you."

"No!" I put my hand in front of his camera. The last thing I needed was to end up with my face plastered across the Web.

"Fine. Where's Scott?" He swung his camera around and started tracking the bodies in the pool, looking for Scott.

"He's training, Mr. Smothers. I think now would be a bad time." Lee's voice was gentle but firm.

"Look," Alex said, sounding irritated. "You know the deal—unlimited access. I can talk to him anywhere, anytime. That was the contract we signed."

"Fine. Best of luck to you getting him out of the water. He's got his earplugs in and his head underwater. You were a swimmer, you know the deal—he'll never hear you. Why don't we talk instead?"

Alex hesitated. Then he threw up his hands in exasperation.

"Fine!"

"Joe, didn't Scott have some things he needed you to do?"

Lee winked at me. He was in on the ATAC deal, and I could tell he was giving me a chance to get away from the camera. I was really coming to like him.

"Yeah, I'll see you guys later."

I walked off as Alex started asking Lee a bunch of questions. Alex was seriously beginning to annoy me, but then, I guess that was part of his job. I decided to stay near the pool area, just in case something went wrong. If yesterday taught me anything, it was that even Olympic security was no match for our stalker. Or stalkers.

For thirty minutes, I wandered around poolside, trying to keep a subtle eye on Scott and all his belongings. I wanted to make sure no one tampered with him or his stuff.

"Excuse me. You. Excuse me!"

It took me a moment to realize someone was talking to me. I turned around to see one of the female swimmers from the American team heading in my direction.

"You're Scott's friend, right?"

"Guilty as charged." I smiled. She was tall, with dark hair and a handsome face. Like everyone around here, she was in incredible shape.

"I'm Isabelle," she said. "Isabelle Helene. I swim the

four hundred meter." She stuck out her hand to shake.

"Joe," I said. "I'm Scott's personal assistant."

We stood there for a second, both of us silent. She looked down at the ground. Girls can't help themselves around me sometimes. It's my curse. The patented MoJoe.

"So how's training going?" I asked. I knew how to handle girls who were nervous around me. Just be friendly, make conversation, and let them calm down. Who could blame them for being starstruck around me?

"Great. How's Scott doing?"

"He's doing good. I mean, it's stressful and all, but he's dedicated. It's been interesting, getting to work so closely with him. I've really been—"

"That's great," she said, cutting me off. "I'd love to get to talk to Scott sometime. He's been so busy recently, we just haven't been able to spend much time together. Do you know where he'll be tonight?"

"Do you two normally spend a lot of time together, Ms. . . .?"

Alex and his camera were back. Isabelle seemed quite happy about it. She turned and smiled big.

"Isabelle. Isabelle Helene. And not that it's any of your business, but yes—Scott and I have spent a good deal of time together. You know, when you're doing something like this"—Isabelle waved her arms around, indicating the arena all around them—"you end up establishing some pretty intense . . . *relationships.*"

The way she said that last word definitely seemed to imply that she and Scott were more than just teammates or friends. What the heck? Had Scott dated Lexi, and Isabelle, and Elisa? Or was she making this up?

"In fact," Isabelle continued, "I was hoping to see Scott tonight, but I couldn't remember where we were supposed to meet. I was just asking his personal assistant here . . ." Isabelle drifted off, clearly waiting for me to tell her Scott's plans for the evening.

"What? Oh, I don't have my planner on me. I'm afraid I don't know anything without my planner." I tried my best to look helpless.

"Well, maybe I'll come find you later and you can tell me then." The way she said it, it sounded more like a command than a possibility.

"So, Ms. Helene, how are you feeling about the Olympics?"

"Feeling? This isn't about feeling. This is about winning. And I am prepared to do whatever it takes to win. That's my motto in life. Whatever it takes."

Something about the insistent way she asked about Scott turned me off from Isabelle. She seemed to really like Scott—in fact, she seemed to think they might be dating—but I didn't trust her. Could she be his stalker? But if she liked him so much, why would she try to hurt him? Although, liking Scott could be a good reason to hurt Lexi . . . This was just too confusing. I decided to put her down as a suspect, though, just in case.

Suspect Profile

Name: Isabelle Helene

Hometown: Los Angeles, California

Occupation: Professional swimmer

Physical description: Isabelle is tall. Like, really tall. I had to look up, so I'd guess she's six-one. And if she wasn't a professional athlete, she'd probably have a career in modeling. But there's something a little crazy in her eyes. Maybe it's just the dedication and focus it takes to be an Olympic athlete . . . or maybe it's something else.

Suspected of: Her questions about Scott definitely bordered on stalker-ish. But I have a feeling she wouldn't hurt him. But maybe she'd hurt Lexi? Or maybe I'm just beginning to suspect everyone?

Motive: If she really is as hung up on Scott as she appeared, Lexi would definitely be her number one enemy.

Suspicious behavior: Nothing specific yet. But I'm keeping my eye on her. "Whatever it takes" is definitely the attitude of someone who would stop at nothing.

The rest of the day passed without incident, though I did spend a fair amount of time dodging both Isabelle and Alex. Finally, around six p.m., I headed home on the scooter I had convinced ATAC to send me. It was better than having a car in LA—I could zip between traffic and get home in record time. In fact, I beat Scott by a full thirty minutes. I used the time to check out the house. Everything looked legit: no broken windows, no forced locks, no psychotic stalkers hiding in the shower.

I flopped down on the couch, and was about to put my feet up on the table when I remembered—all white. No putting my feet up anywhere, not unless I wanted Scott to spend the night cleaning the house again. Carefully, I sat up and made sure there was nothing on me that might stain the couch. Then I dug the all-white remote out of the all-white basket by the table, and turned on the television.

Or at least, I tried to. It wasn't working properly. No matter what channel I tried, all I got was static. That was weird. I called Vijay for some tech support—since we had him, I might as well use him, right? But my phone was all static as well.

Something was definitely going on. This was creepy. I heard Scott's car pull up, and I ran to meet him at the door.

"Hey, Scott—something's going on. The TV signal is all screwed up, and so is my phone."

"Don't worry about that," Scott said as he brushed past me. "This is LA, the smog will do that sometimes. Gets so thick it interrupts everything. Call the cable company and see what they say. I've got to hop in the wave pool—traffic was so bad I'm already seventeen minutes behind schedule."

I followed Scott through the house. He shed clothing as he went, his Olympic tracksuit flung on the floor. He really must have been in a hurry! I'd never seen him put so much as a piece of paper down out of place. Soon, he was in just his bathing suit, and we were in the training area of the house.

The wave pool was a much smaller pool than his regular one. It was designed for building strength. It had a motor at one end that generated waves, strong or weak depending on the setting. The whole point was to swim against the current.

As Scott started stretching, I noticed a weird smell in the air. It was like a thunderstorm. *Maybe that's it,* I thought. *Maybe we're about to have a big storm.* But that didn't seem right. I hadn't seen a single cloud on my drive home.

Suddenly, it clicked.

"Scott, no!"

I ran. Scott looked up just in time for me to tackle him, head on. His foot couldn't have been more than two inches from the water.

"Ow! What the heck? Get off me!"

We wrestled for a moment. My arm slammed painfully against the tile, and I could tell I'd have a wicked bruise in the morning. It didn't matter. Nothing mattered, so long as I could get him away from the pool. The last thing I wanted was for both of us to fall in together.

When we rolled into the wall of the training area, I let go of Scott.

"What is your problem?" he yelled.

I lay there for a second, panting. Then I pulled my keys out of my pocket.

"Watch."

I tossed the keys into the pool. There was a sound like bees buzzing, and a giant electrical spark leaped along the surface of the water when they hit it.

"Someone's tampered with the motor. The whole thing is one huge electric chair."

Scott's stalker had just upgraded from creepy to killer.

CHAPTER

NANCY

THINGS THAT GO BOOM IN THE NIGHT

"So, one of us stays with Lexi at all times. No matter what. Right?" I looked both Bess and George in the eye, to emphasize how serious I was. After the scares of the last few days, who knew what might happen next.

Bess screamed. "Eyes on the road! Eyes on the road!"

As though I hadn't already looked and made sure there was no traffic coming. She was a just a little nervous because she'd had too much coffee.

"Agreed?"

"Right! Someone with Lexi at all times. We got it." That was George. She was always much more level-headed about these things.

"What are you going to be up to?" said Bess.

"Whoever's harassing Lexi was able to get into the

women's locker room and leave a note in her locker. So we're looking for a woman, probably a fellow athlete, right?"

"Or a member of the press," said Bess.

"Or one of the janitors," added George.

"Right." I paused for a moment, thinking it all through. "Well, regardless, the one place where we know for sure her stalker has been—has actually, physically touched—is Lexi's locker. So I'm going to start by looking there."

I merged onto the freeway and into downtown LA traffic. Man, was this city one big snarl. A traffic jam in River Heights meant that there had been an accident somewhere, or that someone's dog had escaped and was playing in traffic. In LA, jammed just seemed to be the normal state of affairs. It was when traffic moved that things felt weird.

Finally, though, we made it to the Olympic Arena. After we got through the doors, we split up. Bess and George headed over to watch Lexi train. I headed for the locker rooms. I wasn't 100% sure my pass would get me in there, but I'd learned that the best thing to do in a situation like that was to act like you were supposed to be there, and people rarely challenged you.

I pulled out my cell phone. Not only did I have a call to make, but this was another good trick I'd learned. If you were on a phone when you breezed by, people often felt too awkward to try to talk to you, and you had a good reason "not to hear them" if they did.

"Hey—is this Vijay?"

"Talking to you live in mono. The infamous Nancy Drew, I presume?"

I had to laugh. I'd never met Vijay in person, but from what Joe, Frank, and George all told me, he seemed like a great guy. And he was definitely fun on the phone.

"That's me. Although I don't know how 'infamous' I am."

"The only person to ever crack Frank and Joe's cover? The best detective east of the Mississippi? Or is it west? I can never remember where River Heights is."

"You've been doing your homework."

"Information is my job, lady friend. So what can I do you for?"

"I hear you've got cameras hidden throughout the arena."

"I can neither confirm nor deny these rumors," said Vijay, his voice deadpan. I laughed again.

"Well, if you do have cameras, do you think you could check the footage for the women's locker room, and see if anyone has been messing around with Lexi's locker?"

"If we had put cameras around the space, I would have been the one to do it. And if I had been the one putting up cameras, I wouldn't really have been able to get into the women's locker room, would I?"

"Right. Good hypothetical point. Well, could you

Blush, I had long ago learned, had many uses.

Sadly, the front of the locker held no information—or rather, too much. A quick glance showed dozens, if not more, sets of fingerprints. There'd be no way to figure out who had brushed it in passing and who had broken into it. Besides, the person who'd broken in had probably used gloves to do it. I imagined that would probably be the case, but you always had to try the obvious answers first, just in case. I'd cracked more cases due to stupidity on the parts of the perpetrators than anything else.

Lexi had given me the combination, so I opened the locker. Not much was in there—her street clothes and a few books. I rifled through the pockets and flipped through the books, but I didn't find much of anything. A photo fell out of one of the books when I opened it, or rather, half of a photo did. I picked it up off the floor. It was of Lexi. Someone had torn it in two. It might not have been anything . . . but I wanted to ask Lexi about it anyway. You could never be too careful.

The rest of the day was uneventful. Lexi's dad had to run some errands, so we promised to drive Lexi back to the Starlet when her training was over. Bess, George, and I spent most of the day in the stands, watching Lexi destroy her opponents. She seemed a shoo-in for the gold medal—if she lived to make it to the actual games.

"So how are you feeling?" I asked Lexi, in between one of her matches.

look for any footage of someone tampering with her fencing blade?"

"That would be more doable. But it'd take a while. Not even sure where I'd start to look. I guess I'd have to watch the fight, then follow the blade back through the various cameras, to try and see at what point someone sharpened it. That will take a while. I mean, *would* take a while. If I had hidden cameras in the arena. Which I can neither confirm nor deny."

"Thanks, Vijay. You're the best."

"Peace out girl scout."

As I slipped the phone into my pocket, I realized had totally worked. I had been so distracted by talking to Vijay, I hadn't even noticed when I'd breezed right by security and into the women's locker room! Nancy Drew one, Olympic security zero.

The locker room was just endless rows of red metal lockers and wooden benches. It looked like a slightly upscale gym. This was the behind-the-scenes part the arena. It was no frills—a place for serious people do serious work.

Lexi's locker was number 173. From the outside looked just like all the others. Red metal, a little s than I was, maybe eight inches wide. I dug throu purse and pulled out a makeup compact. After look around to confirm I was alone, I flipped it op out a makeup brush, and began to dust for fi

"All right. Leg burns a little, but I think it'll be fine."

I couldn't believe she was back to fencing just a day after being injured. But I guess you didn't make it to the Olympics without being dedicated.

"Well, you seem to be doing just fine, even with the injury."

"Yeah. It's going to take more than a little flesh wound to slow me down."

"Ha! We'll be cheering for you in the stands."

"Thanks." The smile slipped from Lexi's face for a second. "Thanks for everything, Nancy. I think I'd be a total mess if I didn't know you were out there, watching my back."

I squeezed her shoulder. "Get back out there and do what you do best. Leave the detecting to me."

I walked back over to Bess and George. It felt good to be working on a case for someone I cared so much about.

"Excuse me, miss? Miss?"

I turned around to find a camera in my face.

"I'm Alex Smothers. I'm with Sportztime—perhaps you've watched our shows?"

I hadn't, but I'd definitely heard of Sportztime. They were one of those Web start-up companies that had actually managed to challenge television and newspapers. Lots of people went to them for their sports news. And Alex Smothers was the brainchild behind it all, as well as their star reporter.

"I saw you talking to Lexi Adams, and I was wondering if I could ask you a few questions?"

"Of course you can," Bess had sidled up next to me. She put on a big smile for the camera. George joined her on my other side. "We're old friends, the three of us. We go all the way back to River Heights Elementary School."

"Oh, great! This is great stuff. I'm doing a documentary piece on Scott Trevor, and as his girlfriend, I'd love to get some more information about Lexi. May I?"

He pointed to the camera. I hesitated, then nodded. It would probably help our cover to look like a bunch of innocent childhood fans.

"Great. Rolling in three . . . two . . . one . . . So, tell me your names and how you know Lexi?

"I'm Nancy, Nancy Drew. And we were in Mr. Angstrom's third-grade class together."

"George Fayne. I was in the same class."

"Me too! And my name's Elizabeth Marvin. But everyone calls me Bess."

"Great. So, do you think it's appropriate for two Olympic athletes to be dating each other? I mean, doesn't that take something away from the innocent spirit of international competition?"

What? I thought. That was certainly a loaded question.

"I think it's great that two focused, dedicated people with so much in common have been able to find each other," I replied.

"Yeah," added Bess. "They're in love. It's totes cute."

"Great, this is great. So if it's not inappropriate, why do you think they hid it for so long?"

"Probably because they knew that creeps in the media would be all over them if they knew," George said. She has a knack for saying the things the rest of us just think.

Alex laughed, a loud, fake bark of a laugh.

"Do you think this will negatively affect their performance in the games? Are they really focused on their performances, or are they too busy being 'in love' to take all of this seriously?"

"I think that if they do poorly at the Olympics, it will be because their relationship was a reason for guys like you to harass them constantly!" said Bess angrily.

"You know what, we actually have to go," I said. I'd had enough of this guy's attitude. Why is it that journalists always have to look for a scandal or something wrong?

"Well, thanks for your time, girls. Check out Sportztime tonight. I think I'll be running some excerpts from this interview tonight. And if you ever have more to say, here's my card." He handed us three of his cards. On the front they read ALEX SMOTHERS—PRESIDENT AND CHIEF CORRESPONDENT, SPORTZTIME.COM—FORMER OLYMPIC GOLD MEDALIST.

I slipped one into my pocket. My fingers brushed against the photo I had put in there earlier. I'd forgotten to ask Lexi about it. I looked around and saw her packing up her stuff. Bess, George, and I headed over to her.

"Ready to go?" she said as she slung her bag of gear over her shoulder.

"You don't want to change or anything?" I asked.

"Nah. I'm kind of avoiding using the lockers as much as possible. You know?"

I nodded.

"How was talking with Alex?" Lexi asked.

George snorted. "He's a piece of work!"

"I know, right?" said Lexi. "He's so irritating. I guess it's his job and all, and Lee says that all the press is going to be great for Scott, but I wish he'd just buzz off."

We headed out to the street. At the door, I hesitated. I looked both ways. It was getting dark now, and I didn't see the car anywhere.

"Uhh . . . anyone remember where I parked?"

Lexi laughed. "Some things never change, eh?"

"Luckily, Bess and I have taken care of this problem."

It took me a moment to figure out what George meant. Then I remembered: the remote starter they had installed in the car! I hadn't had a chance to use it yet. I pulled out my keys and clicked the big button they'd put on my key ring.

BOOOOOOMMM!

Two hundred feet down the street, a giant ball of fire erupted into the sky.

CHAPTER **12**

FRANK

RESTRAINING ORDER

You'd think that being a secret agent on a deadly mission in the middle of the Olympics would have to be exciting all the time, right? Well, you'd be wrong. This was crunch time for the athletes, and if they'd been focused before, now they existed for only one reason: to train. I was a ghost in the arena, pretty much the only person there without something to do.

Of course, that did have one benefit: No one noticed me keeping an eye on Scott from a distance. Although, truth be told, I could have been standing two feet from him, staring at him, the whole day and I don't think anyone would have noticed that, either. Even the towel boys and janitors seemed to be feeling the pressure. Everyone was moving at about twice their normal speed.

And there I was, sitting in the bleachers. I almost wished I had a book with me. Except I knew as soon as I opened it we'd be attacked by motorized snakes or Scott would spontaneously combust or something. To kill time, I got out some pens and found a long piece of cardboard. I spent an hour stenciling "Scott Trevor—Biggest Fan!" on one side of it. I might as well do my best to stick to my cover story, even if it made me look totally lame. I even drew a little pool, with a stick figure swimming through it. When I was done, it looked like an overeager second grader had made it, but I was still pretty proud.

The sign got me some attention. Scott gave me a thumbs-up, and Lee came over with some official Olympic swag—a tracksuit, a handkerchief, and a bunch of promotional programs and posters. Mr. Adams gave me a dirty look when he saw the sign, but for the most part, he seemed to be keeping a wide berth away from anything related to Scott. Nancy said that Lexi had had a talk with him, and it seemed to have had some effect. Publicly, at least. Who knows what he was capable of behind the scenes? I watched him closely, but though he gave Scott dirty looks at every opportunity, I never saw him get close to Scott.

Making a sign wasn't exactly wrestling bad guys to the ground, but at least it gave me something to do. For a while. Then it was back to just staring out at the arena.

"Biggest fan, eh?" said a voice behind me suddenly.

I looked over my shoulder to see a woman in one of the Olympic athlete jackets standing a little behind me. Her hair was wet from the pool, and because she was standing on the bleachers and was already quite tall, she towered over me. Joe had pointed her out to me yesterday—Isabelle Helene. He'd briefed me on their short interactions, and I wasn't surprised that my sign about Scott caught her eye. *Maybe*, I thought, *this will be a good a chance to size her up*.

"Yeah—I won a contest!" I did my best to sound like an eager high school kid, excited to get to talk to a real live Olympic athlete.

"So how many world records does he hold?" Isabelle asked. She sat down hard on the bleacher behind me, and put her feet up next to me.

"Three! In the hundred meter, two hundred meter, and four hundred meter freestyle." I'd done my homework. If she thought she could stump me that easily, she had another thing coming.

"So what are his times?"

"Uh . . ." I thought for a moment. I knew I'd read them, but could I remember them on the spot? Then it came to me. "46.91 seconds, 1:42 seconds, and 3:40 seconds."

"Humph." Isabelle sniffed audibly, clearly displeased that I'd gotten them right. She was silent for a moment. Then she gave a short bark of a laugh.

"All right, 'Biggest Fan,' whose record is he about to beat for most gold medals by a single athlete?"

My mind blanked. I knew he was about to break the record, but I had no idea who was the current record holder. I tried to think of a good guess. Mark Spitz was up there, I knew. And Jesse Owens. Isabelle was staring at me, a self-satisfied smile growing on her face. I took a gamble.

"Mark Spitz?"

"Nope! Ha! I knew you were just some poser."

She got up to walk away. I can't say I was sorry to see her go. She was some piece of work. But I was curious.

"Hey!" I yelled at her retreating form. "Who was it?"

Isabelle didn't respond.

But our conversation had alerted all of the journalists to my presence. They were all looking to get some background footage of the Olympics, and with my sign, I guess I made a great visual. Over and over again, I got asked how excited I was to be there, if I thought Scott would break the gold medal record, etc. Hours passed. The arena got darker as the sun set. People began to leave. I was so used to the reporters that when a pretty redheaded woman with a camera in front of her face came up to me and started asking questions, I didn't think anything about it. At first.

"So you're Scott's 'Biggest Fan,' eh?" she said.

"Yup. That's me! See?" I held up the sign for the

camera and gave a goofy grin. If I thought of it as an acting exercise, this wasn't so bad.

"Yeah, I know kid, I saw you on the television the other night. Frank . . ."

"Carson. Frank Carson."

"Right. Carson. Well, mind if I ask you a few questions?"

"Go right ahead." She was a little more no-nonsense than most of the journalists, and she hadn't given me her name, or the name of the station she worked for, but a lot of them were like that. This was their job; they weren't here to socialize.

"So what's Scott like in person?"

"Well, so far he's been really nice to me. He let me sit in on his training session, and we've talked about swimming a lot. I'm a swimmer, too, actually, and—"

"Great. That's great. I hear he can be really difficult to be around sometimes. A prima donna, you know? Kinda spoiled? What do you think about that?"

"What? I don't—I mean, he's never been like that around me. I'm sure anyone would be stressed out if they were competing in the Olympics, though."

She seemed irritated at my response. She huffed loudly.

"Yeah, but he's totally obsessive-compulsive, right? A neat freak?"

"He's . . . clean, but I don't think it's weird or anything."

The gears in my head were spinning. Something about her hair, her voice, and the questions she was asking suddenly clicked in my head. "Wait a second! You're Elisa, aren't you? His former manager?"

"What has he said about me? How do you know who I am?"

She sounded angry, but she never put the camera down. I knew better than to respond while she was still filming. I stood up and started to walk away.

"Hey! You come back here. We're not done yet."

I ignored her—but her yelling attracted someone else's attention.

"Elisa? What are you doing here?!" Scott was fresh out of the pool and still dripping wet. He looked out of breath—and very, very angry.

"This is a public space, Scott. I can be here if I want to. In fact, I was just talking to a friend of yours." She jerked her head in my direction.

"Whoa—wait, no way. I was walking away. I didn't say anything to her." The last thing I wanted was for Scott to think I was conspiring with Elisa. Luckily, Scott wasn't paying any attention to me.

"I have a restraining order. Do you really want me to call security on you?"

Elisa hesitated. Then she made an exaggerated show of looking at her watch.

"Gee, Scott, wish I could talk longer but I've got to go.

I've got a dinner deal with my agent about the book. I'll be sure to send you a signed copy when it comes out."

With that, Elisa turned tail and nearly jogged out of the building. She was gutsy, I had to give her that. But even she didn't want to deal with the LAPD on high alert.

"Why were you talking to her?" Now that Elisa was gone, Scott seemed to notice me again. He didn't seem any less annoyed without her around.

"See, I was sitting here with the sign, and all these journalists came up, and I didn't know who she was until she started asking all these questions about you being obsessive-compulsive, and that kind of stuff."

"She said what? I'm going to call my lawyer."

He reached down to pull out his phone before he realized he was only wearing his bathing suit.

Right as I went to offer him mine, a giant explosion sounded from outside the building. The ground shook. Some of the front windows of the arena shattered, and a hail of glass rained down.

"Earthquake!" yelled someone, I couldn't see who. They were wrong, though. This wasn't an earthquake. This was a bomb.

People were screaming. Thankfully, the arena was mostly empty, or we could have had a deadly stampede. I didn't even notice I was running for the door until I was squirming my way through the milling crowd of confused and frightened people.

I burst out of the door to find Nancy, Bess, George, and Lexi standing in stunned silence, staring off into the dark. Up and down the street, car alarms were going off. Two hundred feet away, the remains of Nancy's car burned brightly, sending terrifying shadows up against the walls. I could smell the burnt metal from where I stood. I could only hope no innocent passersby had been near the car when it exploded.

CHAPTER **13**

JOE

A SECRET RENDEZVOUS

"All my CDs were in the trunk. Including my signed collection of every disc The Royal We ever put out," said George.

"My sunglasses. My Armani sunglasses. The ones I rebuilt myself after I found them at a flea market for two dollars," Bess added.

"My car. What am I going to tell my father?" whispered Nancy.

"Tell him it was impounded for one too many parking tickets. He'd believe that." Bess giggled. Nancy lifted a pillow off the edge of the couch and tossed it at her— but she smiled. It was the first time any of us had smiled in hours.

After the explosion, the police had grilled Nancy,

Lexi, Bess, and George for more than an hour. Originally, they'd wanted to take them into custody, but a little quick thinking on Frank's part—and a few calls to our father—had gotten them off the hook, although the police were still investigating. I doubted they were going to find any evidence at the scene. By the time we'd finally gotten a taxi to take us back to Nancy's hotel, all that was left of her car was a smoking heap of twisted metal.

But the police had at least given us the night off from watching Lexi and Scott. The Olympics was only two days away, and tonight was the official Opening Gala. Lexi and Scott, and all of the athletes, were the guests of honor. There would already be more security than at Fort Knox, and now that the police knew that Lexi and Scott were being targeted, they would each have their own private security detail. Getting close to them would be as difficult as getting close to Britney Spears. Even ATAC would have had a hard time swinging getting us through the doors, let alone Nancy, Bess, and George. And the way things had been going the past few days, none of us wanted to separate.

"So what do you think?" I asked Nancy.

"Well, we don't have any great suspects. Elisa and Alex have the know-how. Everybody has a bit of a motive. But no one feels like a lock."

"No, I meant—local news or cable?" I wanted to see

what the coverage of today looked like. Nancy laughed.

"Let's try cable. I think I saw a CNN camera outside right before my car blew up."

We flipped around, but most of the coverage of the Olympics ignored the bomb going off. I guessed they'd probably tried as hard as they could to keep it out of the news, the way they did with protests over human rights violations in different countries. The Olympics were all about athletic competition, international cooperation—and selling tickets. The last thing they wanted was bad press. One of the things you learned, being a secret agent and all, was that the news on the television was rarely the full story, or even half of it. What little coverage of the explosion we saw spun it as an "unexplained traffic accident," and didn't mention the fact that it took place a mere two hundred feet from the Olympic Arena.

"Wait! Stop. That was us!" Bess yelled.

I flipped the channel back. There were Bess, Nancy, and George talking to Alex Smothers. The familiar Sportztime logo was in the corner, and beneath them were their names in Sportztime's font.

"Do you think this will negatively affect their performance in the games? Are they really focused on their performances, or are they too busy being 'in love' to take all of this seriously?" said Alex's voice.

"I think that if they do poorly at the Olympics, it will

be because their relationship—," said Bess. Then the camera cut away.

"What! That's so not what I said. He took that completely out of context!" Bess was on her feet, yelling at the television. Normally, she was so calm and chill. I'd never seen her flip like this.

"Hey. Relax. That's what these guys do," said Nancy. "He's a professional gossip. Everyone knows not to believe a word that people say on his show."

"Yeah, but now Lexi and Scott are going to think I'm out to get them!"

"I think Lexi, at least, knows which side you're on. And by the time all of this is over, so will Scott," I said.

"Whatever. Let's turn it off."

I ordered pizza from room service, and we talked over our suspects for a while.

"I think we're dealing with two people—at least," said Frank.

"I agree. It doesn't seem like any one of our suspects could—or would—be doing all this on their own," added Nancy. At least, I think that's what she said. Her mouth was so full of pizza it was kind of hard to make out what she was saying.

"Let's make a spreadsheet," said George. "We need to get a full picture of all of our suspects, and who might be working together." She pulled out her laptop and everyone gathered around.

"I think it's Elisa," said Bess. "You can't trust these journalists. She hates Scott. And she used to date him or something, right? So she probably hates Lexi. Plus, she knows all about cameras and tech stuff."

Suddenly, my phone rang. I read the display.

"Speak of the devil. Why is Elisa calling me?" I held up a hand and everyone grew quiet while I answered the phone.

"Hi, Elisa." I was about to ask why she was calling, but Elisa cut me off.

"That explosion—that was about them, wasn't it? Scott and Lexi? There isn't much on the air about it, but I called around." She sounded scared. And guilty.

"I can't really talk about that with you." Who knew if this was just another ploy to try and get me to bad-mouth Scott on tape.

"Look, Joe. This isn't—I mean, I don't—I just . . ." Elisa went silent.

"Hello?" I said after a few seconds. I was afraid she'd hung up.

"There are some things I didn't tell you before. You have to believe me, I had no idea this would happen. I have some information. I need to give you something."

Was she crying? What was going on?

"Sure. Of course. Where?"

"There's a parking lot about a half mile down the street from Scott's place. I can't go any closer, because of the restraining order. I'll meet you there in thirty minutes."

I was about to tell her I was in the city, not at Scott's place, but she hung up before I could say anything. When I tried to call her back, her phone was off.

"Looks like I'm headed out. Thank God ATAC got me that scooter."

"Do you want someone to come with you?" Nancy offered.

"What, are you going to follow me in a cab? I'll be all right. I don't trust Elisa, but I don't think she's going to hurt me. Besides, someone needs to do the thinking part of this." To tell the truth, our conversation had been going around in circles, and while I hoped they would figure something out, I was getting itchy just sitting around.

"All right," said Bess. "But be careful. I'd hate to see that cute face end up on missing persons posters." She leaned in and kissed my cheek. Man, do girls love it when you put yourself in danger!

I leaped onto my scooter and took off through LA traffic. I would probably just make it in time.

Or be fifteen minutes late. By the time I pulled onto the long, mostly empty road that led to Scott's house, I'd had to weave my way through two traffic jams and one five-car accident. I don't know how people manage to get around that city on a daily basis!

The parking lot was dark when I got there, but I could make out one car sitting in the corner farthest from the street lights. As I drove up to it, my headlight illuminated the inside of the car, and I saw Elisa sitting in the front seat, looking at her lap.

I stopped my scooter and hopped off. Elisa remained in her car. I pulled open the passenger side door.

"Hey," I said.

Elisa didn't look up. Something about the angle of her head was wrong. My heart started to pound.

"Elisa. Elisa! ELISA!" I yelled her name. She didn't respond. I tapped her shoulder, and she sagged against the door. Her hair moved, and I could see a vicious line of black and purple bruises around her neck. Someone had strangled her to death. Our number one suspect was now our number one victim.

I pulled off my T-shirt and put it around my right hand. I didn't want to leave behind any more fingerprints. I did a quick check of the car. Aside from a whole lot of take-out Chinese containers, it was pretty much empty. In Elisa's pocket, however, I found a portable flash drive. She said she had something she wanted to give me . . .

I grabbed it and got out of the car. A quick call to the same police officers we'd spoken with that afternoon, and the LAPD were on their way. I didn't have the time to stick around and talk to them. Someone was making their move, and I only hoped I could stop them before the body count got any higher.

I checked my watch. A little after ten. The gala should have ended, so I called Scott.

"Where are you?" I said as soon as he picked up.

"We just got back to my house." He must have driven right past me. Then I realized what he had said.

"We?"

"Lexi's here with me. She was so freaked out by what happened this afternoon, she didn't want to go back to the Starlet."

"Stay where you are. Don't let anyone in the house. I'm on my way."

I flipped my phone closed. I needed to make sure they were all right. And I needed Scott to tell me what he'd been hiding. What was really going on between him and Elisa? Why had he fired her? Was it worth killing her over? And what was on that flash drive?

"Joe? What's going on?" I barely it made through the door before Scott and Lexi were right on top of me. They both look scared. Scott was so nervous he hadn't even bothered to put away the bag of swag that he had received at the gala. It was sitting in plain view on the table, with a watch and a bottle of cologne pouring out of it. He was too upset to clean—it was a new low for him.

"Elisa is dead."

"What??" Scott collapsed into a chair.

I explained what had happened in the last hour.

"It's all my fault," he whispered into his clenched hands. It sounded like he was crying. Lexi stood behind him with a hand on his shoulder.

"I need to know what was going on between the two of you, Scott. Why did you fire her? She hinted that the two of you were in a relationship. Tell me the truth, or we might never know why she was killed."

Scott sat silently, shaking his head. It was Lexi who spoke.

"They *weren't* dating. Scott hired her because she looked like me. We were trying to keep our relationship a secret, and when photos of Scott with a 'unnamed woman' started popping up in the tabloids, Scott thought we could continue to fool everyone. When that didn't work, Scott asked Elisa to pretend they were dating. It was all because of me. I was afraid if my father found out we were dating, he'd never let me see Scott again."

She stopped.

"So what happened? Why'd you fire her?"

"Because she stopped pretending," Scott spoke up. "She really fell for me. I had no idea—until she outed Lexi and me to Lexi's father. She was trying to break us up. I fired her the next day. Ever since, she's had this vendetta against me. But it's my fault—I asked her to pretend to be in love with me. I got her involved with all of this. And now . . . I've gotten her killed."

Scott's voice broke. He started crying. I looked away as Lexi put her arms around him.

"Scott . . . I promise you, we'll find out who did this. This isn't your fault. She called me. She was involved in something. She wanted to help you. The only person responsible for this is the person who killed her. Not you."

He didn't answer. I knew it wasn't much, but I hoped at some point he'd be able to hear what I'd said. In the distance, I heard sirens approaching, and knew the cops were coming to investigate Elisa's body. I checked the security alarms on the building and said good-bye. Lexi promised she'd look after him. Then I headed back to Nancy's hotel.

It had already been a long day. It looked like it was going to be an even longer night.

CHAPTER 14

LET'S GO TO THE VIDEOTAPE

In exactly one day, two of my friends were either going to be competing for gold medals, or—the way this case was going—they were going to be dead. It's not the kind of thought that leads to a good night's sleep. After Joe got back from meeting up with Elisa, or what was left of her, I think it's safe to say that none of us slept well. Except maybe George, who can sleep anywhere, anytime. And I heard the snoring to prove it.

"Pass the . . . you know. That." Frank pointed at the bottle of ketchup at my elbow. He seemed to be about as awake as I was. Silently, I handed the bottle to him, and watched as he covered his eggs, toast, and hash browns in a thick layer of ketchup.

131

"Dude, you want some breakfast with that ketchup?" asked Joe.

"No," said Frank.

We all ate in silence for a few more minutes. We'd all met up at the Moonbeam Diner again for breakfast to go over our plans one last time. George and Bess had already left—they were going to be watching over Lexi today. Bess had her pepper spray on her and George had something she'd made out of parts of her old computer and a few big batteries. She said it was like a Taser. I pitied the fool who tried to hurt Lexi on their watch. That freed up Joe and me to go talk to Vijay. I was eager to meet another ATAC agent in the flesh. Plus, I was hoping he'd be able to decode what was on the flash drive Joe had found on Elisa's body. George popped it into her laptop last night, but she'd realized pretty quickly that the encryption was beyond what she could handle without her full computer setup. As for Frank . . .

"So, ready for your close-up?" Joe ran his hand through Frank's hair. "They're going to need to send you to wardrobe first. And makeup. Maybe the plastic surgery department."

Frank threw a ketchup-covered piece of potato at Joe. He was not looking forward to spending his day at an all-day shoot with Scott and Alex. It gave him a chance to watch them both, but it meant a lot of sitting around, and a lot of being interviewed—two of his least favorite things.

While Joe picked potato out of his hair, I signaled the waitress for the check.

"All right boys, time for us to get out of here." I was eager to get on the road. This was our murderer's last chance to stop Scott and Lexi from competing in the Olympics, and I was pretty sure that whoever they were, they weren't sitting around having a food fight. I gulped down the last of my coffee as we headed out the door.

"Here, take this," said Joe as he thrust a helmet in my direction. "Hold on to me as tight as you can. Don't worry; my rock-hard abs can take it."

"Rock-hard abs? And here I thought that was the milk shake you had for breakfast settling."

Joe laughed, and we hopped on his scooter and zoomed into downtown LA. I was still mourning the loss of my car, especially after all the work that George and Bess had put into it. But I had to admit, there was a freedom to the scooter that I enjoyed. You felt like you could go anywhere. Maybe when this was all over I'd look and see if they had a sky blue model.

We were at Vijay's hotel in no time.

"Try not to drool," Joe warned me as we parked the scooter. "Vijay definitely scored the best place this time around."

"Wow, you're not kidding. This makes that resort we stayed at in Florida look like a cheap motel."

Like everything else in LA, the hotel was glass and chrome everywhere. But this place had infused all of that with some of the old-school Hollywood glamour. Everything was art deco fabulousness. Bess would have died to have gotten a look at the place.

As the elevator doors closed around us, the orchestral music faded out, and a voice crackled over the stereo.

"Ah, Ms. Drew. How nice to get to meet you in person."

I looked around, startled.

"Vijay?" said Joe.

"I had some free time, so I hacked into the elevator's cameras and audio equipment. I could get used to living in a place this swank."

Swank was definitely the word for it. The elevator doors opened into the largest hotel room I'd ever seen. Joe tossed the flash drive to Vijay and gave me the five-minute tour. He'd promised me a ten-minute tour—and the place was big enough to give a thirty-minute tour, at least—but Vijay had the encryption cracked in five.

"Looks like a video file. Let's go to the big screen." Vijay typed a few commands on his computer, and a movie screen began to lower from the ceiling. At the same time, black shades began to rise up from the floor and block all the windows. Within moments, it was dark as night inside.

Grainy black-and-white footage of Scott appeared on the screen. It was clearly from lots of different cameras, at lots of different times. Scott falling into the pool, Scott freaking out about something, Scott cleaning obsessively.

"This is all the footage Elisa is—was—releasing to the television stations," said Joe. "Why would she need to show me that?"

"Maybe this wasn't what she wanted to show you," I said. "What if she just had this in her pocket?" I felt my hope draining away. This wasn't going to be the clue that broke the case after all. A few minutes later, the footage ended. Vijay reached down to turn off the projector, when something else popped up on the screen.

YOU KNOW WHAT TO DO WITH THIS, it read.

"What is that?" I blurted out.

"Do you think that was a message from Elisa to me?"

"No," answered Vijay, "I think that was a message from whoever gave Elisa that footage."

"Gave her the footage? But I thought she said she'd filmed it herself."

"That's what she said," said Vijay. "But that's not what this tape is telling me. Look, this footage is from seven different cameras." Vijay pointed to a new screen he had pulled up that had a breakdown of the different segments of the video and what they had been shot on. "Not one of them is the camera she's been using for any of the reporting stuff she's done in the last year. Someone made this tape for her."

"That's what she wanted to tell me!" said Joe, excited. "Someone else was leaking information to her. And whoever it is is probably the same person who made that tape of Scott sleeping."

"And they made that voice-edit they played over the national anthem, too," said Vijay. "Looks like it was done on the same editing software."

"Something about those words . . ." I started to say, but stopped. I couldn't think of it.

"What is it?" said Joe.

"I don't know. But something about those words was familiar." It would come to me at some point. But for right now, it was just a buzzing sensation, like a fly stuck in my brain. There was something about those words that I should know.

"Any hint on who made the tape?" said Joe.

"Nope. They scrubbed it pretty good." Vijay whistled to himself for a moment, shutting down the computer projector and opening up the screens. "Anything else I can do for you guys?"

"Yeah," I said. I pulled out the photo I had found in Lexi's locker. In all the craziness, I hadn't had the time to ask her about it. "I dusted this for fingerprints, but I didn't find any. Joe said you might have some more sensitive equipment."

Vijay smiled. "You're my new best friend. Now I've got a way to justify my new toy to ATAC. Throw it on the laser scanner over there."

Vijay pointed to what looked like a pane of glass hovering above a small table.

"This uses lasers to detect oils and markings that traditional powder or ink methods can't find. If there's anything on this photo, we'll see it."

The machine sprung into action and a red light filled the room. A few seconds later, a message popped up on the screen.

"Nothing," said Vijay. Then he paused. "Or rather, no fingerprints. Whoever did this was clever—they washed it down using chlorine to destroy the evidence. But this scanner can pick up chemical residue signatures."

"At least that lets me know someone did tamper with it, even if it doesn't tell me who." I put it back in my bag. "I'm going to have to ask Lexi about it."

"I think we're done here anyway, right V?" said Joe.

"Unless you want to stay and watch *Revenge of the Nerds III* with me?"

"Thanks for the offer, but . . ."

"Yeah, yeah. A superspy's work is never done. Go on, get out!"

"I like him," I said to Joe as we rode the elevator back down to the lobby.

"Vijay?" Joe winked at me. "He's a real nerd."

The elevator shuddered to a halt.

"I heard that!" Vijay's voice came out over the loud-speaker. Joe and I laughed.

"Just playing with you!"

"Humph. Well . . . I'll let it go this time." The elevator started back up. We laughed all the way to the scooter.

Joe dropped me off at the Olympic Arena so I could find Lexi. He wanted to head back to the Starlet, to look over the spreadsheet we'd made last night and see if any of it connected with what had happened last night. He left the scooter with me, just in case. He said he'd catch a taxi back.

It didn't take me long to find Lexi inside. All I had to do was follow the sound of her father's voice. I found her standing by the fencing mats, drinking water. Her father was gesticulating angrily.

"I'm not sure we really have time for you to take a break right now, Lexi. The opening ceremony is tomor-row!"

"Dad. I've been training for four hours. If I don't take a break, I'm going to pull a muscle. Do you really want that to happen?"

Even though she was facing away from me, I could tell Lexi was exasperated. All of it: the stress of the

Olympics, the death threats, Elisa's murder—it was getting to her. I'd never seen her so much as disagree with her father before. Now it looked like they were about to get into a fight.

I stepped in between them.

"Hi, Lexi! Hi, Mr. Adams!" I said brightly, in an effort to break the tension. "Lexi, could I talk with you for a minute?"

"Sure," she said without even looking at her father. He threw up his hands and stomped off, while Lexi and I took a seat on the bleachers.

"How are things going?" I asked.

"Well, the biggest day of my life is tomorrow, someone just killed my boyfriend's ex-pretend-girlfriend, and I'm about to kill my father. How do you think it's going?"

She gave a laugh that was on the edge of tears.

"Hey," I said, looking her straight in the eye. "You're going to get through this."

A tear leaked out of her eye. I put my arms around her and she buried her head on my shoulder.

"Oh, Nancy," she mumbled. "What would I do without you?"

When her eyes were dry and she had managed to compose herself, she pulled back and sat up.

"I should find my dad and get back to training," she said.

"Wait. Before you go, I had a question for you."

I rummaged around in my pocket for the photograph, and handed it to her.

"I found this in your locker."

"Oh, yeah. I had that hanging on the inside of the door. But where's the other half?"

"This is how I found it. What was in the rest of the photo?"

"I'd gone to visit Scott at one of the Olympic trials. It was a photo of me and him and a couple of his teammates. We liked the photo so much, we got the photographer to send us both copies. Do you think . . . Is this another threat?"

"No," I said. I didn't want to worry her. "I'm sure it was just an accident."

"Right. I'm not dumb, Nancy." She smiled, a weak smile, but a real one. "But I'm not worried. I know you'll be able to handle it."

Lexi squeezed my hand and stood up. "I've got to get back to training. I'll see you later tonight."

Once she was gone, I called Frank. I told him about the torn photo, and the chlorine tampering that Vijay had found on Lexi's copy of it. Since he was at Scott's house all day for the filming, I asked him to try and find Scott's copy of the photo. Maybe someone just wanted Lexi "out of the picture," literally. Or maybe the other half of the photo held some clue to our killer's identity.

CHAPTER 15

FRANK

BLOWING MY COVER

We'd spent all day filming Scott around LA: his favorite stores (a couple of vintage places, mostly down hidden alleyways where you'd never expect to find anything other than a Dumpster and a mangy cat), his favorite restaurants (man, could he eat! I guess exercising that much gave you quite the appetite, 'cause he seemed to always have the munchies), and his favorite "date spots." I couldn't believe how many questions Alex could find to ask Scott. By the time the day was over, he must have known Scott better than anyone else in the world. And though I still found him irritating, he didn't do anything particularly suspicious. He did trot me out in front of the camera at nearly every location, to ask me how I felt that Scott's favorite color was green, or if

I liked Thai food as well. The most excitement we saw all day was when Alex tripped while walking backward filming us and nearly broke his camera. Aside from that, nada.

For the second half of the day, Scott was going to be training. Alex would get to ask him questions occasionally, but Scott insisted there was no way he could take the entire day before the games off from training. This, I figured, was my chance to look for that picture Nancy had mentioned.

"I'll be with you guys in a minute," I yelled, as Scott and Alex headed down the hall to the gym area. "Too much coffee." I smiled and pointed toward the bathroom.

I shut the door behind me and counted to ten. I listened at the door. I heard nothing. Quickly, I opened the door and scanned the room. It looked like I was alone. I walked down the hall in the opposite direction from where Scott and Alex had gone, away from the gym and toward Scott's bedroom. I'd never been inside it before, but I figured if he was going to keep a photo of him and Lexi anywhere, it would be there.

Inside, his bedroom was as immaculate as the rest of the house: white walls, white carpet, white blanket on a white bed. There was a huge wall of books on one side, and he'd even gone to the trouble of having them all rebound with new, white covers. But there was one thing in the room that wasn't white: a framed picture on the nightstand, right by his bed. It was facing away from me, so I couldn't make out who was in it, but even before I got close, I felt certain this was the right photo.

I nearly ran across the room in my excitement. Maybe this would finally be the clue that made this case make sense. Just as I lifted the picture off the nightstand, I felt a breeze behind me and heard fast footsteps approaching. I turned, but not in time.

BAM!

Next thing I knew, someone had their arms around me and I was flying through the air. Luckily, I landed on the bed, but whoever had just tackled me was right on top of me. I drove my elbow back into their stomach.

"Oomph!"

Whoever this guy was, he was made of steel. Hitting his stomach felt like hitting a brick wall. But I'd knocked some of the air out of him, enough that his arms loosened and I was able to break his hold. I squirmed free of his arms, but his entire weight was still on me, pinning me to the bed. I dropped one leg down on the floor to give myself some leverage, and then pushed as hard as I could, flipping us over so that he was against the bed. I stood up on the soft mattress, which was hard to balance on, and got my first good look at my attacker.

"Scott?!"

"Who are you? Why are you doing this to me?"

I was so shocked that I was completely unprepared for Scott's low kick, which knocked my legs right out from under me. We ended up tangled on the bed. Scott tried to get me in a headlock. I grabbed his arm and slipped out from under him. It wasn't easy trying to fight someone you didn't want to hurt!

"Stop it! Scott, this isn't what you think it is!"

I tried to get my ATAC badge out of my pocket, but Scott must have thought I was reaching for a weapon, because he tackled me to the floor and knocked my hands. This time, there was no mattress to cushion the fall. My back was going to be bruised for weeks. Scott was kneeling on top of me, pinning my arms to the ground.

"Right. So you weren't just going through my stuff? And yesterday you weren't talking to Elisa about me? And you haven't been sending me death threats all along?"

"No! Ugh!"

He hit me in the face. Man, Scott could throw a punch. I had to stop this before he ended up seriously hurting me, or I was forced to hurt him in self-defense. There was only one thing to do.

"I'm with ATAC! American Teens Against Crime!"

Scott paused, his arm raised to punch me again.

"Joe is my brother! I'm in deep cover, so no one—

not even you—would know I was working to protect you."

"How do I know you're telling me the truth?"

"How else would I know about Joe? Or ATAC? But if you don't believe me, check my pocket—you'll find my ATAC badge there."

Without letting me up, Scott slid his hand into my pants pocket and fished out my badge. Once he had it in hand, Scott leaped to his feet.

"Oh man, I'm sorry!"

He reached down to help me up. Once I was standing, I leaned against the wall and felt my face. Man, was I going to have one heck of a black eye. But nothing felt broken. Scott looked horribly embarrassed.

"I swear, I had no idea. I wouldn't have hit you—it was just, I'm under so much stress, and when I saw you going through my stuff, I figured . . ."

"It's okay. This is one of the risks of going undercover. You have to lie to your friends just as much as to your enemies."

"I'm sorry I tackled you though. And punched you. What were you doing in here, anyway?"

"Looking for this."

In our scuffle, the picture had fallen to the ground, facedown. Luckily, the frame hadn't broken, or we would have been rolling on broken glass.

I lifted it up and turned it over.

There was Lexi, with her arm around Scott. And right next to him, on the other side, was that swimmer, Isabelle Helene. And boy, did she look pissed. That's when it all came together in my head. Isabelle liked Scott. Therefore, she had reason to hate Lexi. She hadn't ripped Lexi out of this photo—she'd ripped out herself and Scott! And the chlorine residue Vijay found on it wasn't used on purpose to destroy her fingerprints, it was just the chlorine from the swimming pools!

"What's so important about that photo?"

"Someone tore it in half and stole part of it from Lexi's locker. We think it's the same person who was threatening her. We knew it had to be someone with access to the entire Olympic Arena, since they were able to tamper with Lexi's locker and her fencing equipment. And I'm pretty sure that it's Isabelle!"

"No!" Scott gasped.

"I know she's your friend and teammate, but—"

"No, that isn't it! She told me today that she and Lexi were getting closer, and that she wanted to stop by Lexi's hotel and surprise her tonight. You know, wish her luck before the games started. So I told her Lexi was staying at the Starlet Grand Hotel."

"Uh-oh. We've got to get someone over there now."

I called Nancy. She'd been at the Olympic Arena. With any luck, she was still with Lexi.

"Hey, Nancy. Lexi's in danger. Isabelle is after her

and has her address. I can't explain now. Is she there with you?"

"No—she headed back a little while ago. I only have the scooter, so I couldn't give her a ride. I'm right outside Vijay's place. He was going through the tapes from the arena, trying to see if he could find who was messing with Lexi's stuff, so I thought I would check in. But Joe headed back to the Starlet earlier—maybe he's still there!"

"I'll give him a call."

"I'm going to try and call Lexi to warn her."

"All right. Stay in touch."

I hung up and dialed Joe.

"Code Red Joe. Isabelle Helene is headed to the Starlet, and I'm pretty sure she's out to kill Lexi."

"Damn! I went out for dinner. I'm running back, but it's going to take me a while."

"Get there as fast as you can.

CHAPTER **16**

JOE

ROAD RAGE

I was running before I even got off the phone with Frank. I'd decided to go out for a long walk before dinner, in the hopes that some brilliant answer would come to me. And now, one had come—over the phone, when I was possibly too far away to make a difference. I tried to reassure myself. Maybe Lexi wasn't even at The Starlet. Maybe Frank was wrong. Maybe, maybe, maybe.

I'd gone all of three blocks when something caught my eye: a motorcycle dealership on the corner, which was just closing up shop. I'd never gotten to ride the bike we had on our last mission, except piggyback on Frank. But I had a lot of experience with the scooter, and ATAC did give us "emergency credit cards" for situations just like this.

Three minutes and a whole lot of money later, I was kick-starting the engine on a brand new Kawasaki Ninja. This was a bike built for speed. It was bright yellow, and to ride it you bent so far forward you were almost lying down. It was a sharp, aerodynamic needle of a vehicle. It had such a sweet engine, it wasn't even that loud, it just buzzed like a trail of hornets in my wake. Five minutes later, I pulled up in front of the Starlet.

I left the bike behind a bush in front of one of the side entrances. I couldn't take the time to give it to the valet, and I figured I might need it soon, so I couldn't just park it somewhere around the block. Hopefully, it would still be there when I got back.

I entered the lobby, only to run smack into what seemed to be every tourist in LA.

"I'm so excited about the games! I just can't wait to see those Ryan twins compete. They are too cute!"

"Is this your first time at the Olympics?"

"I just want to see a movie star! I swear, if I don't see Brad and Angelina before the week is out, I'm asking someone for my money back."

It was a sea of people in red, white, and blue shirts. With the Olympics starting tomorrow, everyone was in town, and the Starlet had more guests than it could handle. And all of them, it seemed, were standing in my way.

"Excuse me. Sorry! Pardon me."

I tried to push my way to the elevators, but once I saw the line for them, I gave up. It would take me longer to get to Lexi's floor than it had taken me to get to the hotel!

Then I spotted the entrance to the emergency stairs, partially hidden behind a potted plant. I yanked the door open and started running. Nancy had been on the thirteenth floor, and Lexi was on the floor above her, so that meant I had . . . a long way to go.

I hit the stairs in what must have been record time. If there were a StairMaster event in the Olympics, I would have been a shoo-in for a gold medal.

"Hello? Lexi!"

I pounded on her door. There was no answer. *Maybe,* I thought hopefully, *she isn't even here.*

I put my ear to the door. There was a squeak on the other side. It could have been anything: the wood settling, someone walking in the hallway, my imagination. Or it could have been a muffled scream.

Better safe than sorry, I thought.

I stepped back, took a deep breath, and delivered a wicked sidekick to the door.

CRASH!

The door flew inward. Lexi was standing directly in front of it. Behind her stood Isabelle with one hand clamped firmly over Lexi's mouth. The other held her wrist behind her back. Behind them, Bess and George were tied up on the floor.

Before I could get more than one foot in the room, Isabelle threw Lexi right at me. She slammed into my chest, and I managed to get my arms around her and keep us both from hitting the ground, but it was a close call. A split second later, Isabelle bodychecked us on the way out the door, and we went down in a heap. *Damn!* I thought as I hurtled into the floor, *she's strong.*

"Are you all okay?" I asked Lexi as I disentangled myself from her. I looked at Bess and George. Aside from a bad bruise on Bess's cheek, and a ragged cut on George's arm, they looked fine.

"I . . . I think so. She forced the door open and—"

"Look, if you're not hurt, I need you to cut them free and call the police." I tossed my pocketknife at Lexi. "Does the bathroom here have a lock?"

Lexi nodded yes.

"Good. Lock yourselves in and wait for the police. I don't care who else shows up—don't let anyone in. I'm going after Isabelle."

Lexi nodded. I helped her up and took off running out the doorway.

"Be careful!" I heard her yell. Then I heard the sound of two doors slamming. One came from Lexi's suite—it must have been the bathroom. The other came from in front of me, and I would bet anything it was Isabelle heading down the emergency stairs.

"Stop!" I screamed down the staircase. I could hear

footsteps below me, and I thought I caught a glimpse of her as she turned a corner, but that was it. No response.

Right, I thought, *because after all she's done, she's going to give up just because I yelled "stop."*

Looked like it was time to break my stair-climbing record. At least this time I was headed down, not up. But despite everything, I couldn't close the gap between us. I couldn't even keep up. By the time she hit the last step, I was a floor and a half behind her.

Thankfully, nothing she could do could get her through the lobby any faster. I heard angry shouts as she tried to push her way into the crowds. I exited the stairwell just in time to see her leaving by the main entrance.

It's got to be here somewhere, I thought. I looked around. There! Forty feet from me there was a service door that led out to the other side of the building. It must have been the door I'd hidden my bike next to. I pushed my way over to it, and was outside in just a few seconds.

Success! It was the right door, and my bike was still there. I leaped on and spun out into the street. I turned the corner to the front entrance of Starlet Grand, just in time to see Isabelle disappearing inside a low-to-the-ground imported silver sports car. The kind of vehicle that you saw in movies about royalty in Monaco. I groaned internally. There went my hopes that she was driving some sort of compact or station wagon. It would be an even race between my bike and her car.

Or at least, it would have been in any other city. But in LA, smaller was better. I could outmaneuver her any day of the week. As soon as we hit traffic, I had her.

That is, if I could keep up with her that long. She drove like a NASCAR racer, shifting and weaving through lanes of traffic. She ignored red lights and stop lights, and left screaming pedestrians and swerving vehicles in her wake. It was all I could do to keep her in sight and avoid hitting anyone.

Any minute now, I thought, *we'll hit some famous LA traffic.*

But the minutes kept passing, and the streets stayed clear. Of course, she was from LA—she knew how to navigate the city.

Suddenly, Isabelle pulled a hard turn to the left. I heard her tires squeal as she spun out of control. Or at least, it looked like she was out of control. A second before she hit the wall, she threw the car in reverse, spun the wheel in the other direction, and was suddenly heading back the way we'd come. She'd just done a U-turn without ever going below sixty miles an hour. And unfortunately, I'd seen most of it in my rearview mirror as I flew past her.

I watched her turn left down a one-way street and disappear. I didn't have time to wait for traffic anymore.

I had to get to her before she managed to lose me. This was her city—it was only a matter of time before she managed to shake me.

If I tried to catch up with her now, I was bound to lose her. What I needed to do was get in front of her. Instead of heading back and following her, I took my next right, hoping the street would run parallel to the one she'd taken. I edged the bike faster and faster, watching the speedometer hit one hundred and keep going. When other cars appeared, I rode up onto the sidewalk. When there were pedestrians, I cut back to the street. I skipped through a narrow gap between a fruit vendor and a parked car.

CRACK!

My left side mirror snapped off like a wishbone breaking. The bike wobbled for a second, but I managed to keep going. There went any chance I had of returning the bike and getting my money back when this was over. Maybe ATAC would let me keep it . . .

One block passed by. Then another. As I reached a third intersection, I decided this was it. I'd either gained enough ground, and could turn down this street and intercept her, or she was gone and I needed to call ATAC for reinforcements.

Damn, I'm good, I thought as I pulled a hard left turn that put me within inches of her silver car door. Even over the noise of the wind and the traffic, I could hear her scream of rage. I accelerated rapidly, putting myself just in front of her and to the left. And just in time, too, as she slammed her car to the left in an effort to side-swipe me. As Isabelle's car passed behind me, I slowed down suddenly, until I was right next to her passenger side door. With a quick wish for good luck, I grabbed the handle, yanked the door open, and threw myself in.

Before I had a chance to even gain my bearings, Isabelle was on me. She wasn't giving up without a fight. Her right hand slammed straight into my head.

"Get out of my car!" she screamed.

It was all I could do to brace myself against the door-frame to keep from being pushed out right into oncoming traffic. I twisted my neck this way and that, hoping to break her grip, but she had my head palmed in her strong hand. I could feel myself being inched out of the car.

"Give it up. The police are on their way." I had no idea if that was true, but it was the sort of line that people fell for. Isabelle didn't respond; she just pushed harder against my head. This was starting to hurt. One of my legs was completely out of the car now, and I could feel the surface of the road scratching off the tip of my shoe.

Well, I hate to fight dirty, but . . .

I had no time to play fair. I shifted my head again, until her hand was partially over my mouth.

Chomp!

I bit down as hard as I could on her hand. Isabelle screamed, and I tasted something warm and salty in my mouth. She yanked her hand back, pulling me with her. My teeth were still clamped down on her hand. I couldn't let go yet. I needed to distract her for just a second more.

My foot groped along the floor of the car. While Isabelle was distracted trying to get me off of her hand, I yanked the seat belt over me and clicked it into place. Then I let go of her hand and pounded my foot down on the brake.

Even with my belt on, the whiplash felt like it was going to tear my head right off. My chin slammed into my chest, and then rebounded back, driving my skull into the seat. For Isabelle, the impact was even worse. Her head slammed straight into the steering wheel. By the time the car had come to a complete halt a few seconds later, she was barely conscious. But even then, she put up a fight. As I reached over to unbuckle her belt and see how seriously she was injured, she threw a weak punch at my face. I blocked it easily, and checked her pulse to make sure she was okay. I could hear a siren in the distance—police or ambulance, we'd be out of here soon.

"Get off me!" Isabelle whispered in a labored voice.

"It's over, Isabelle. Lexi and Scott are safe, and the only games you're going to be competing in are the ones they play in prison."

"I would never hurt Scott. I love him."

"Yeah—you love him so much you've been trying to kill him!"

"No! We were made for each other. Everything I did, I did for us. I had to get rid of those other girls—Elisa, Lexi—so he and I could finally be together. We would have been the perfect couple."

She had no reason to lie at this point. And despite being crazy, she sounded sincere.

"So you haven't been harassing Scott? You didn't try to electrocute him?"

"No!" She was so angry, she struggled to get up again. "I would never hurt him."

The police and ambulance arrived then, so I didn't have any more time to talk to her. Turns out she was banged up, and she'd have one heck of a concussion, but she was going to be okay. Or at least, as okay as she was before the accident. Sounds like things were a little off in her head way before this accident.

But if what she said was true, that meant someone else was out to get Scott. Which meant he was still in danger.

I tried to call Frank, but his phone rang and rang before finally going to voice mail. Strange. I tried Nancy. Voice mail again.

A chill passed through me. Something was wrong.

CHAPTER 17

NANCY/FRANK

BLINDSIDED

NANCY

At Vijay's, I paced the apartment, trying to will Joe to call me. How long could it take him to get back to the hotel? I tried Lexi twice more, but each time I got her voice mail. Bess and George both had their phones off. Bess usually kept her phone off, so I could see her forgetting to turn it on, even in the middle of a mission like this one. But George lived on her phone. If it was off . . . I didn't want to think what that could mean.

"Vijay, can you pull up that footage again?" I needed to do something to distract myself.

"But of course," he said with a slight curtsy. I rolled my eyes, but I had to admit he knew how to make me smile.

I watched the few minutes of footage of Scott again. It was all familiar stuff that had been shown to death on the news and various tawdry talk shows. Why had Elisa wanted to show this to us? I looked to see if perhaps Isabelle would be hiding in the corner of one of the shots, some shred of a reason that would connect this footage with her. But there was nothing. This had nothing to do with her. And since she was the one behind the attacks, that meant this was nothing. Just a random video that Elisa had in her pocket that night.

Then the words popped up again. YOU KNOW WHAT TO DO WITH THIS.

It certainly made it sound as though someone had given this footage to Elisa. But how would Isabelle have gotten ahold of it? Maybe she was stalking him, but whoever took these clips had complete access to Scott's life. It seemed almost impossible that Isabelle had done it.

And what was it about those words? Something about them tickled my mind. Had someone said them to me before?

Then I realized it wasn't what the words said. It was how they looked.

"Vijay!"

"Nancy?"

"Did you record that footage of Bess, George, and I being interviewed?"

"Of course." He sounded personally offended, as

though I'd asked him whether he ever brushed his teeth.

"Can you pull that up for me?"

Vijay reached over to the keyboard and started tapping away.

"No—not here. On another monitor. I want to see them side by side."

Vijay gave me a quizzical look, but he did it. I was on to something, and I knew it. I only hoped it wasn't too late.

"Look!" I pointed at the screens.

"Yes, the three of you do look lovely."

I whacked Vijay on the arm.

"No, look at our names."

Our names were printed on the screen, below each of our faces. The fonts on both screens were identical. And it wasn't just a coincidence.

"That's why those words were familiar! That font—it's the font Sportztime uses in their logo and promotions and everything. It's on everything they do."

Vijay had snapped to attention and was typing at the speed of light.

"You have a good eye, Nancy. You're right. It's a proprietary font, named Sportztime, natch. And it was created by one Alex Smothers."

While he was talking, the video of our interview had kept playing. We hadn't watched the rest of it, but something caught my attention.

"Wait—Vijay, rewind that a few seconds!"

Vijay clicked a few times, and the file jumped backward. Alex appeared on the screen, midsentence.

". . . the verge of breaking my own world record for most gold medals won by a single athlete. How does that feel?"

The camera cut to Scott, but I didn't hear his response.

The font was created by Alex. Alex had lots of recording and camera experience. Thanks to the exclusive news series he was doing about Scott, he had full access to Scott's life. Alex had everything he needed to be the one behind Scott's attempted murder. And now, he had a motive: Scott was about to replace him as the most decorated Olympic medalist ever.

And Frank and Scott were alone with him. Alone with a desperate man who knew that tonight was his last chance to get rid of his greatest enemy, his nemesis, Scott Trevor. I had to warn Frank—if it wasn't already too late.

"Frank! Oh thank God, you're alive."

"Nancy?"

"Is Scott with you? Where is Alex?"

"No—they're in the pool area, doing a final shoot. What's going on?"

"It's him, Frank! Alex! He's the one who's been after Scott all this time."

FRANK

Before Nancy even started explaining, I was up and running down the hallway. Nancy wouldn't call me unless she was certain that Alex was responsible. My whole body hurt—Scott had managed to do a number on me while we were wrestling. But I tried to ignore the twinges of pain as I raced to the training center.

"How did you figure it out?" I huffed into the phone as I ran.

"The font on the footage Elisa wanted to give Joe? It was the font Sportztime uses, and it was invented by Alex! And then I found out that Alex was the current record holder for the most gold medals won by an Olympic athlete."

"Giving him the perfect motive!" I remembered Isabelle asking me that question, and I could have hit myself for not going to look it up. It all made sense now. "I'm almost to the pool now. I just hope I'm in time."

I slammed open the door to the training area. Scott was on the ground on the side of the pool. Was he unconscious or already dead? There was no way I could tell. Alex was standing over him.

"Get away from him!" I screamed.

I ran toward them. My only plan was to tackle Alex, like Scott had tackled me earlier. Whatever he was about to do, I had to stop him. But Alex was quicker than I thought. He bent down and grabbed something off the floor. Right as I was about to leap, he swung his arm in a wide arc.

The world went white. A searing pain spread across my face. My eyes! I couldn't see anything. By the smell, I could tell he had thrown chlorine or some other pool chemical at me. I felt him shove me hard as he ran past, his footsteps retreating off into the distance. I screamed in pain.

N A N C Y

"Frank? Frank! What's happening?"

I heard him scream in the background. He must have dropped his phone, because everything had become muffled and far away.

"Call 911!" I told Vijay. I didn't want to hang up on Frank, but they needed help now. I only hoped the police would be fast enough.

"Nancy?" Frank's voice, soaked with pain, suddenly reappeared on the line.

"Frank, what happened? Are you okay? Is Scott?"

"He threw something at me. I can't see anything, and he's getting away. I'm trying to find Scott now."

If he got out of the house, our chances of catching him were slim. I slammed my fist down on the desk, making the monitors jump.

The monitors!

"Vijay, pull up all the cameras in Scott's house, now! Frank, can you move?"

"Yeah. But if I can't see anything, what good will it do?"

"You put cameras in every room of the house, right?"

"Pretty much."

"All right. I'm going to be your eyes."

By this point, Vijay had all the cameras live. I could see Alex in the kitchen, rifling through the shelves. *What is he doing?* I wondered. Then, when he pulled out the paper towels and matches, I realized it.

"Frank! He's in the kitchen. He's planning on burning down the house, with you and Scott in it. Can you get Scott out?" I could see from the monitor that Scott wasn't moving.

"No. He's alive, but he's unconscious, and I can't carry him like this."

"All right. Listen to me. Seventy feet in front of you is the door to the hallway. It opens into the pool room."

"I'm heading for it now."

"After the door, it's about twenty-five feet to the stairs." As I spoke, I watched the little figures on the screen: Frank, making his way slowly out of the training room, one hand on his phone, the other rubbing his red and tearing eyes; and Alex, moving quickly throughout the house, making small piles of paper towels. There wasn't much time.

"Now I want you to go ten more feet, and turn right. There's going to be a small—"

"Ow!"

"Table. Sorry about that, you're moving faster than I expected. There's a bronze statue of a swimmer on the table. Pick it up."

"What's Alex up to?"

"He's approaching the hallway you're in. Five feet beyond the table, you'll find a doorway. The door should be open. Duck inside it."

F R A N K

I could feel the smooth metal of the statue in my hands, but if Nancy hadn't told me it was a swimmer, I'd never have been able to tell. How did blind people learn Braille? Or do anything? The pain had begun to recede, but I still couldn't see a thing. I held still and waited. I could hear Nancy's breathing on the phone. There would be only one chance at this. I couldn't fight Alex blind, and once he finished placing the little piles of paper around the house, it would be the work of thirty seconds to run around, light each of them, and leave Scott and me to burn to death.

I heard the muffled progress of footsteps coming

down the hall toward me. It was hard not to jump out. They sounded so close. Surely he had to be in front of me now. But I waited.

"Now, Frank!" Nancy yelled on the phone.

I leaped forward, swinging the statue in front of me at what I hoped was head height. I hit something hard, and heard the sound of a body slumping to the floor.

"Nice shot!" Nancy yelled. "He's down for the count. You did it!"

CHAPTER 18

JOE

GOING FOR GOLD

"And Scott Trevor takes the gold! That's his third gold medal in this Olympics alone, and he is now officially the most decorated Olympic athlete of all time, breaking the record held by one Alex Smothers. And that's a whole other story right there, isn't it, folks?"

Amid the cheering in the hotel room, I switched off the sound on the television. The last thing we needed was another recap of the footage of the police bringing a blind Frank and an unconscious Scott and Alex out of Scott's house. The media couldn't get enough of the story. Or of Isabelle's attempt on Lexi's life—and a traffic helicopter's footage of the high-speed chase that followed, starring yours truly. One paper had dubbed them "The Gold Medal Murders" after both Lexi and Scott had taken the gold in their first events.

"Scott! Scott! Scott!" Nancy, George, Bess, and Frank were chanting. Frank's eyes were still red from the chemical burns Alex had given him, but his sight had mostly returned and the doctors said he wouldn't have any lingering effects.

"Anybody else hungry?" I asked.

"Yes!" Nancy yelled.

"Let's go back to the Moonbeam, one last time," added Bess.

We'd gone to the Moonbeam nearly every day since we'd wrapped up the case. It had become our regular hangout. And since our case had very nearly gotten Bess and George killed, ATAC had been eager to pay for all their expenses afterward. Just one more perk of being a superspy: free lunch. Which reminded me, I had a surprise for them.

"I'll call a cab," said Nancy.

"Wait, Nancy—catch!" I pulled a small box out of my pocket and tossed it to Nancy. Across the room, Frank smiled.

"What's this?" said Nancy.

"A thank-you from ATAC."

Nancy pulled the ribbon off the sky blue box and popped the lid. She lifted out a key.

"Joe," she said in an excited voice, "is this—"

"A key to your new sky blue convertible, paid for by ATAC? Yes."

"It's a hybrid, too. Just like your old one," Frank chimed in.

Nancy screamed with joy. Losing her car had been one of the worst parts of this case, and I knew she'd been dreading explaining it to her father. ATAC was so grateful for her help, though, that it hadn't been hard to talk them into replacing it for her. It wasn't quite as cool as one George and Bess had fixed up by hand, but it was the best I could do.

"All right," Nancy said, "you boys take the gold in classiness. Let's go get some food."

FRANKLIN W. DIXON

THE HARDY BOYS

Undercover Brothers®

INVESTIGATE THESE TWO ADVENTUROUS MYSTERY TRILOGIES WITH AGENTS FRANK AND JOE HARDY!

#25 Double Trouble

#26 Double Down

#28 Galaxy X

#29 X-plosion

#27 Double Deception

#30 The X-Factor

From Aladdin
Published by Simon & Schuster